A HIDDEN RUBY

A HIDDEN RUBY

A MARSDEN ROMANCE BOOK FOUR

DAWN BROWER

MONARCHAL GLENN PRESS

CONTENTS

This one is for all those readers that begged me for Noah's story. I hope it lives up to your expectations.

PROLOGUE

"I no longer wish to live... Without my love, I have nothing."

Rubina Leone St. John, the Duchess of Huntly meant those words. Without Noah... Her head fell forward hitting the palm of her hands. Tears streamed down her face. How could she go on without the only man she'd ever loved? If Paolo Fonte, Duca d'Sordillo, told the truth, her husband was dead.

"Don't be dramatic, Rubina." He held his hand over his heart. "On my honor, I will always take care of you."

She lifted her head and stared at him through hooded eyes. What a fool. Did he honestly believe she'd willingly stay with him? Her heart would always belong to Noah. No other man would fill the empty void his loss left behind. Slowly, she stood and faced him. With all the strength she had left, she spit in his face.

"You'll never take the place of my Noah." She returned to her seat. Rubina had better things to do with her time than deal with Paolo. He proclaimed to love her, but he'd kept her a prisoner for months in a tiny room. Only coming to visit her so he could stare at her while declaring his love. You don't imprison someone you supposedly love.

Paolo pulled out a handkerchief and wiped his face. "You'll regret that."

"No, I only wish I'd have done it sooner."

He stormed over to her side and lifted her chin, forcing her to look at him.

"*La mia bellezza…*" He stroked his fingers through her hair. "Such beautiful golden-blonde hair—so silky to touch."

Chills ran down her spine and her stomach rolled with queasiness as he touched her. Rubina was not his beauty… She never would be his in any way.

"I don't belong to you. I never have. When will you accept that?" She stared up at him in defiance.

"Never?" He raised an eyebrow. "It is such a very long time, my love. You will learn to love me."

Rubina choked back tears. If Noah was truly dead—it didn't matter. Paolo could do his worst. No matter how hard she tried, her feelings would remain the same. Her heart remained untouched by his false charms...

"*Ti odio.*" She let every ounce of hatred pour out of her. Rubina didn't want there to be any doubt how much she loathed Paolo.

"No, you don't." His sinister laugh filled the tiny room. "My dear, you don't really know what hate is —but you will."

"How did Noah die?"

Rubina needed details to understand how he could really be gone. Her husband was a strong virile man, so full of life. She couldn't truly believe he was —she gulped down a lump in her throat—dead.

"If you must know, someone helped him along to his untimely demise."

"No..." Rubina gasped. "Please—tell me you didn't murder him."

"I'll tell you no such thing. I'm not about to start lying to you my dear." He shoved his hands into his pockets and rocked back on his heels. "It's best you get acclimated to our long life together."

Rubina wanted to die. That would remain true as long as Noah was gone. She had something to take care of before she joined him again. Paolo Fonte's life must end. He would pay for his sins—for hurting Noah. She would live long enough to see it happen. Once she sent him to hell, she'd allow herself to breathe her last breath. She could once again be with her husband. They could spend eternity in each other's arms.

"*Sei un bastardo malvagio,*" she exclaimed. Duca d'Sordillo was an evil bastard. "One day your cruelty will leave this world. On that day I will rejoice."

"Say what you want. Your words mean nothing, but you will come around." He grinned. "Until then, please enjoy the accommodations.

He turned to leave. The door shut with a loud thud. Paolo turned the key, locking her once again in her tiny hovel. Such love he showed her. Rubina stared at the door with disgust. It didn't matter. She had a reason to continue living. Once she found a way to end Paolo's life her mission would be complete. He must pay for the atrocity he caused.

RUBINA GREW WEAK. She barely sustained enough strength to lift up her head. Paolo limited her food to bread and water—barely enough to survive. He was trying to get her to cave—give in to his demands. The evil bastard wanted her to willingly join him in his bed. It would never happen. To betray Noah in such a manner... No, she'd rather die. If she didn't gain strength soon, she'd get her wish.

"Duchessa..."

Her body rocked back and forth, shaking from an unseen force, but she didn't want to open her eyes.

"Please wake up, Duchessa."

Rubina's eyelids fluttered open to gaze into the dark brown eyes of a man she'd never seen before.

"Who are you?" She stared at him, puzzled. Maybe he was a new guard Paolo sent to watch over her.

"I'm here to save you."

Rubina shook and tears streamed down her face. She didn't want to believe it was true. She didn't know how long she'd been a captive in Paolo's home. All she wanted to do was go home—see her father and brother again. They were all she had left in the world. If only Noah...

Rubina cried harder.

"Duchessa, we must hurry."

She tried to swallow a lump in her throat, but it

was too dry. She let her gaze meet his again and voiced her fear. "Are you real?"

He nodded. "I assure you, I am. Can you walk?"

"I'm so weak…"

"We will go slowly. I will carry you if I must."

He helped Rubina to her feet and led her to the open door. She was about to leave her prison. How long had she been locked away from the world?

"Why are you helping me?"

"I work for your brother, Conte Leone." They made their way down the long hallway. He stopped at the top of the stone stairway. "My name is Arturo."

"Damian sent you?"

Her family still believed she lived? Why had it taken them so long to find her? Paolo insisted the world believed her dead—as dead as her husband. No more Duke and Duchess of Huntly—no more beautiful love story.

"I'm afraid not." He lifted her up into his arms. "Everyone believes you are dead. I'm here on a different mission. It's a miracle I learned of your existence."

"Grazie." Rubina hugged him. Her whole body shook with the weight of her emotions. "I feared I'd die locked in that room."

"No need for thanks. I'd do it for anyone." His mouth formed a firm straight line. "What the Duca d'Sordillo was doing to you was wrong."

Rubina didn't want to think about Paolo. She just wanted to get as far away from him as possible. Maybe she'd return to England... She loved her home. Italy still held a special place in her heart, but it also filled her with terror. If she had never argued with Noah, Paolo wouldn't have been able to hold her captive. Her only intent had been to return to Naples and visit her father. As soon as she stepped onto the ship heading toward Italy, Paolo's men had seized her. They took her to his ship and locked her inside. Somehow, he arranged to have the ship she'd been on to sink into the ocean's blue depths—sealing the belief of her death.

"If you're not here to rescue me, then what are you doing in Duca di'Sordillo's home?"

"He is believed to have ties to the Mafioso."

Arturo set her down and scanned the room. He pulled her hand into his and led her outside. They stopped in front of a carriage, and he helped her inside. Once Rubina was safely seated, he flicked the reigns to get the horses moving.

"Somehow it doesn't surprise me. He's an evil

man—and evidently a mastermind in the criminal underworld."

Arturo nodded. "That's what we believed. We had no idea the extent of his criminal activities. Conte Leone sent me to investigate. If he'd known you were here, he would have come himself and ripped Duca d'Sordillo apart."

Rubina didn't doubt it for a minute. Damian was ruthless when he needed to be. He had a high power seat in the government. He hated the Mafioso and sought to eradicate them from Italy. It was turning out to be a daunting task. The Mafioso themselves were shrouded in secrecy.

"Where are we going?"

"Do you know where you are, Duchessa?"

"Please, call me Rubina," she offered. "I owe you my life. To answer your question—I have no idea where I am or how long I've been here."

Arturo frowned. "This is not good, Your Grace." He shook his head. "You are in Sicily near Palermo. It's been three years since the Conte and your father believed you drowned aboard that ship."

Rubina gasped. "No, so long..."

"Your family—they will be so relieved to find you still live. Thankfully, your brother awaits me in a nearby port. We can escape with him and travel to Naples."

Damian was near? The fates had finally decided to step in and help her. If only they'd done so sooner —she might have been able to save Noah. Pinpricks of pain shot through her heart as a vision of her beloved floated before her. She missed him so much.

Arturo urged the horses to go faster. The wind blew through Rubina's hair. Soon she'd be with her brother again, and she could plot Duca d'Sordillo's death. He would pay for his sins. First she'd need to regain her strength. She would not be able to defeat him being so weak.

"We'll be to your brother's ship soon, Your Grace."

"Thank you. I'm so tired... Maybe I should sleep a little bit." Her head fell forward, eyes drifting closed. They flew open as she gazed over at him. "I thought I told you to call me Rubina."

"Yes, Your Grace, but I cannot. Please, stay awake. We will be there soon."

Rubina fought her body's need for sleep. Once they got to the ship and reunited with her brother she could give in. Arturo assured her it was near. Deep breath in, exhale, if she kept reminding herself, it all would still be true. If this was a dream, Rubina never wanted to wake up. Only one thing would make it perfect: Noah—alive and well.

The carriage came to a halt near a small pier. The night sky was dark as pitch with tiny white stars dotting the black canvas.

"Duchessa, we are here." He nudged her forward. "Come, I'll help you board the ship."

"I don't think I can move, Arturo." Her eyes rolled backward, and her eyelids fluttered shut. "I don't have much strength left."

"I will carry you." Arturo lifted her into his brawny arms.

The warmth engulfing her spread throughout her whole body. She'd been cold for so long. He nestled her, letting her head rest on his broad shoulder. It was so nice to be taken care of.

"I don't know if I can ever thank you enough," she muttered.

"Quit thanking me, Your Grace."

Rubina never would. He saved her from a living hell.

"What do you have there, Arturo?"

Damian! His voice was music to Rubina's ears. Arturo hadn't lied. He'd brought her to her brother. Rubina wanted to cry again, but she held it inside.

"I found your sister, Conte."

"What?" Disbelief etched through Damian's voice. "You lie, my sister drowned aboard a ship several years ago."

"No, Conte." Arturo shook his head, jostling Rubina's head forward. "She lives. Duca d'Sordillo has kept her locked in a room for years."

Rubina lifted her head and met eyes that matched her own. In the moonlight, his silver-gray irises glowed in front of her. Damian gasped. "*Dio mio*, it's true..."

"Hello, brother."

Damian rushed forward and pulled Rubina out of Arturo's arms. His hug so tight breathing became difficult. "I can't believe you're here. If I'd known..."

"I know, please, I can't breathe."

Damian let her go, never once taking his gaze off of her. She understood because it all seemed like a dream to her too.

"Rue, oh God—Noah. How are we going to tell him?" Damian rubbed his hands over his face. "He is about to get the shock of his life. We must get to him fast."

"What?" Rubina gasped. "Noah lives? Paolo told me he murdered him."

"I assure you, your husband is alive and well." Damian nodded. He paced back and forth in front of her. His agitation making her nervous. "There's something you should know… He's set to remarry."

"No…"

Noah was hers. No other woman would lay claim to him. She had to get to London and reclaim her husband. How dare he move on when she suffered so much? She'd believed he was dead, and still she didn't give in to Paolo. When she got there, Noah would rue the day he'd ever thought to replace her.

CHAPTER ONE

$\mathcal{N}$oah St. James, the Duke of Huntly took a deep breath and set aside the financial documents he'd been perusing. He rubbed his hands over his face to wipe the exhaustion away. It was already a difficult day, and the sun barely rose in the sky. He'd had trouble sleeping the night before and left his bed while it was still dark outside. Since sleep evaded him, he might as well get some work done.

"You look like hell."

Noah glanced up at his best friend, Liam Marsden, as he strolled into his study.

"I feel like it."

Liam tilted his head to the side. "You're not having second thoughts are you?"

DAWN BROWER

"Of course not. It's the right decision."

It was. Even if it made his insides tighten with dread.

"You don't have to remarry," Liam said softly. "No one knows more than I how much you loved Rubina."

Noah shook his head. "No, it's time. If I want to have children, I need a wife."

He just hoped Pearla knew what she was getting into by marrying him. She said she did, but he doubted she truly understood. Noah had tried being a husband once, and look how it had turned out. Not married a year and his wife fled him in anger, and to her death. If only he'd handled the situation differently...Rubina might still be alive.

"You don't want more?"

"I can't handle it if I lost..." Noah shook his head. "Love has only brought me heartbreak. The ability to love another woman is lost to me."

Pain seared through what was left of his heart. Beautiful and so full of life, Rubina had been his everything. It took him months to begin functioning again. If he let himself love another woman only to lose her—he'd never survive it.

Liam nodded. "I understand. Gemma is my one

14

and only love. I don't know if I could handle losing her."

"You're lucky to have her."

"Is it really fair to Pearla to marry her knowing you will never love her?"

Noah considered Liam's question. Was it fair? No, it wasn't. Pearla understood how he felt about marriage. He hadn't lied to her about anything. She had her own reasons for agreeing to this marriage. Pearla had an inheritance, but lacked the freedom of a matron. She agreed to be his wife and give him a child. Her only requirement was to gain her own freedom. Pearla had dreams of traveling the world, and Noah didn't have a problem letting her. If she wasn't around he was less likely to develop any tender feelings for her.

"Pearla knows what she's getting from me." Bitterness filled his voice as he remembered his first wedding day. This one was sadly lacking and plain miserable. Noah didn't really want to marry anyone, but he had a duty to his title. If he didn't have an heir, the dukedom would revert back to the crown.

"Noah, you look like you are about to walk toward the hangman's noose. This is not a good way to approach your wedding day." Liam frowned. "I don't like seeing you this way."

Noah stood and strolled over to the small bar behind his desk. He grabbed two goblets, filled them with two fingers of brandy, and then placed one in front of Liam. "I assume you would like a drink too."

Liam raised an eyebrow. "It's kind of early isn't it?"

"It's never too bloody early." Noah downed the contents of his glass and slammed it down on his desk. "Sometimes a man just needs a damned drink."

Noah's heart constricted in his chest—it all seemed so wrong. He'd been justifying his decision for weeks. The day had come, and soon he would be married...again. His whole body repelled the very idea, yet he intended to go through with it.

He glanced up at his best friend. Concern etched his features. Noah had no idea how to explain to him what was going through his mind. Liam had the woman he loved. They were blissfully, adoringly besotted with each other. Gemma was the perfect complement to Liam's broody nature. He couldn't be happier for him, but his own misery seared his soul.

"I think you're making a mistake, but if this is what you want, I will stand by you." Liam's lips formed a thin flat line. "But Pearla is Gemma's friend. If she's unhappy..." Liam shook his head. "I'm not telling you what to do. I want you to be happy, and this doesn't seem the way to get there."

"Right. I don't think I know how to..." Noah patted his chest attempting to rub the ache in his heart. "Without Ruby I'm hollow inside. This is the best I can hope for."

"I don't have words. This pain you feel—I don't have anything to draw on."

Noah ran his fingers across the rim of his glass. Maybe he should have another drink. It might numb him enough to get through the ceremony. Liam was right. Pearla deserved someone far better than him. Rubina's ghost haunted him, and she always would. Bloody hell, maybe he would have that second drink after all. He grabbed the brandy decanter and filled his glass to the top.

He took a swig and tipped the glass toward Liam. "I pray you never know the pain of losing your one true love."

"Is this your convoluted way of toasting to the long life of my marriage?"

Noah nodded. "Don't waste it for a second."

Liam sighed. "Didn't plan on it." He studied Noah for several seconds. "I'm only going to say this one more time, and then I'm going to drop it."

"What's that?"

"There is still time to call off the wedding. I can even do it for you. Just say the word."

"The wedding will happen." Noah looked him in the eyes, letting Liam know, without words, his wishes. "This is what I want."

What a joke. No, this wedding wasn't what Noah wanted. If he had one wish, it would be for Rubina to never have died. For her to walk through the door at any moment with her laughter floating around him. He hadn't felt true happiness since he lost her. In lieu of getting his one true wish, he'd settle for a child of his own. Fate owed him at least that much.

Liam picked up his glass and raised it high. "Then how about a real toast. To my good friend Noah. May he find it in his heart to forgive himself and learn to love again. For, without it, happiness will always be beyond his reach, and more than anything he deserves to find it."

Noah stared at him. "That's the worst toast I've ever heard."

"Well, it is all you're getting. Now drink up." Liam downed his brandy and set his glass down. "Now, let's make our way to the carriage. We have a wedding to rush to."

Noah grumbled. "Don't we have more time?"

"I'm afraid not, my friend. It's time to head to the church. The ladies are awaiting our arrival."

Liam would stand beside him as Noah married Pearla. His wife, Gemma, was standing with his intended. They had been planning the wedding for weeks. The banns having been read for the past three weeks in Westminster Abbey, the church where he was going to marry Pearla Montgomery.

Oh, hell. Noah downed the contents of his glass. He did need the liquid courage to go through with it. It wasn't Pearla. No, it was him. Pearla was a lovely woman with gorgeous blonde hair and cerulean blue eyes. In some ways similar to Rubina, but his deceased wife's hair was a rich golden-blonde while her gray eyes turned silver with desire. Noah shook the image from his head. It didn't matter. Pearla was not Rubina. His dear wife, his one true love, was lost to him forever.

It was time to take a new wife.

"Lead the way." Noah stood up. "I'm right behind you."

Liam stopped and looked him up and down. He shook his head. "I'll be with you every step of the way. Just say the word, and I'll take care of anything you need, no matter what it is."

"I can't change the man I've become, Liam. I'm

not sure if I want to." Noah frowned. "Rubina's death made me harder than I ever thought possible. I've lost too much, and I can't afford to lose any more. If anyone else even tries to take what's mine, I won't be able to stop myself from annihilating them."

"Let's pray it doesn't ever come to that."

Noah hoped not because, if it did, he'd lose what was left of his soul.

"How much time do we have to get to the church?"

"We should have been there twenty minutes ago."

"What?" Noah blinked as shock filled him. "Why didn't you say something sooner? I didn't realize what time it was."

Liam shrugged. "I had hoped you'd changed your mind. But, alas, it wasn't to be, so now we need to make haste."

Noah took two quick strides and exited his study. He stopped in the foyer and hollered for Simmons. "I need the carriage brought around. I'm late for my wedding."

"It's already waiting for you, Your Grace."

"Thank you, Simmons. I don't know what I'd do without you."

Simmons nodded and headed for the door,

opening it wide for Noah. Liam followed close behind him, and they entered the ducal carriage.

"How did you get here anyway?" Noah asked. "I didn't see your carriage or horse."

"I had our carriage drop me off. Gemma took it to the church to wait for our arrival."

That couldn't be good. Gemma must know on some level how much Noah didn't want to marry her friend. He respected Liam's wife. Having her displeased with him—it didn't sit well. He'd try to make her understand...later.

It didn't take long, or at least it didn't seem like it, before the carriage halted in front of the church. Noah took a deep breath and hopped out of the carriage. He stopped in front of the steps and stared up at the tall cathedral.

"I said I wouldn't ask again."

Noah's sliced his head left and pinned Liam with a glare. "Then don't."

Liam threw his hands up in the air. "Have it your way. I'll stand by your decision."

Noah nodded and opened the doors wide. He walked with purposeful strides to the altar where the clergyman was awaiting their arrival.

"Let's start the ceremony. I have a lot to do today."

All he wanted to do was get it over with. He ignored the guests filling the pews. They expected more from him, but he couldn't give it to them. This wasn't a love match, and he wasn't about to pretend it was on any level. The vicar nodded his agreement. Music filled the church halls as Noah stared down the aisle.

Gemma floated forward first with light steps in tune to the music. Liam's gaze never left his wife's face. Noah looked back and forth between the two. An ache filled his heart. He'd had that once. Gemma kissed Liam and then hugged Noah. She took her spot on the other side of him. They all turned to watch Pearla march down the aisle on her father's arm.

She was so lovely and perfect. Not one golden hair was out of place. The smile on her face—she looked so happy. Noah didn't understand why. What was there to be so bloody happy about? They reached the end of the aisle. Her father kissed her cheek and sat down in the front pew next to his wife.

Noah grabbed Pearla's hand and led her to the front of the altar. He nodded at the vicar to begin. The vows went by in a blur; if asked, he wouldn't be able to recall saying them.

"If anyone has just cause for these two not to be joined in holy matrimony please speak now or forever hold your peace."

The Vicar's words blended into the background. Noah wanted this done.

"I have some objections."

A soft accented voice reverberated through Noah's ears. His gaze shot toward the location it came from. Everyone turned to see who interrupted the ceremony. Loud murmurs filled the church and echoed back at him, but words failed him. Noah's mouth fell open as shock overtook him. He had to be seeing things. He rubbed his eyes and blinked the blurriness away. His heart beat hard against his chest. How much brandy had he poured down his throat before coming to the wedding? He stared for several seconds, but the apparition in maroon silk kept moving toward him. Noah couldn't believe what his eyes were telling him.

Surely the blonde vision in front of him wasn't…

"Rubina?" he croaked out.

CHAPTER TWO

"*H*ello, Noah dear." Rubina moved closer to him at the altar. She batted her eyelashes at him coquettishly. "Have you missed me?"

Her gaze fell on his new bride. So young, innocent, and perfect in her wedding gown, her gold curls fell down to her shoulders and her blue eyes kept going back and forth between Rubina and Noah. Poor thing chose wrong in deigning to marry her husband. She'd learn Noah belonged only to her.

Wait, Noah couldn't belong to her. His life depended on him hating her. Rubina had to stay focused and not make claims she couldn't make.

"I'm not interrupting anything important am I?" Rubina waved her hand dismissively. "Never mind I see. You're about to replace me. How rude of me to object."

"You're really here." Noah just stared at her.

Rubina could tell she'd shocked him. She shouldn't be upset he moved on. If she were truly dead—no, if she were honest, she didn't want him with anyone else. He said he'd love her forever, and he'd moved on far too quickly for her tastes. Noah would pay for that. She couldn't hurt him more than necessary. She had to protect him. His safety came first. It didn't matter in the grand scheme of things as long as she knew he was whole, healthy, and happy. Rubina would not be selfish at the cost of Noah's life. Paolo would come looking for her, and Noah would be the first place he looked.

"Of course I'm here." Rubina moved in close to him and ran her hand across his broad chest. "Where else would I be but at my husband's wedding. It looks like you had a good turn out."

Rubina smiled brightly and waved to all the guests. Their shocked gasps filled the room. She never did much care for English society. They were all stuck-up snobs.

"I don't understand." Noah shook his head.

Poor man. Rubina should take pity on him, but she wouldn't. Couldn't.

She gazed up at him. His chocolate brown eyes were filled with a mixture of confusion and hope. Rubina cupped his cheek with her hand. "It's simple enough, dear."

She dropped her hand and took a few steps back. Being close enough to touch him was almost too much for her to bear. It had been hellish believing him dead. One thing Rubina understood was the pain of losing the person you loved more than yourself. Noah must have gone through that too. The difference was Rubina couldn't move on and Noah had.

"Nothing is simple about this." Noah clenched his jaw. "I don't understand how you could possibly be here, and I have so many questions."

Rubina smiled. "Oh, but it is, you see. Rumors of my death..." She paused for dramatic effect. "How do I put this...have been a bit exaggerated."

"Noah?" his pretty little bride looked at him, questions in her eyes.

"Pearla, I'm sorry. I don't..." His gaze flew back to Rubina's. "I can't explain this. Please, forgive me."

"It's all right. I understand." She smiled sweetly at him.

Rubina wanted to smack the woman. Bitterness filled her as she watched their exchange. How dare he—Rubina wanted to scream at him with every ounce of frustration building up inside of her. How could he have fallen in love with another woman and forget her so easily.

"Maybe we can move this to someplace a bit more private." A red haired woman suggested. "I'm sure you don't want the ton to know all your personal business."

"I don't mind," Rubina interjected. "What's a little back-from-the-dead experience worth if you can't share it with the world?"

The red-headed tart could bite her damn tongue off for all Rubina cared.

"Rubina," Liam coaxed. "This is a shock. Gemma is right. We should go someplace quieter—at least somewhere you and Noah can figure out what happened. I'm sure you both have many questions."

Rubina tilted her head. "Hello, Liam. I see you're still sticking by your best friend. When I was…away, I thought about you. Considered maybe you shared my grief. Now I see I was the only one who truly grieved."

"It's not like that, Ruby," Liam said.

"Isn't it though?" She raised an eyebrow. "You moved on. Look at each one of you. So happy and content with your picture perfect lives. Who cares what happened to poor Rubina. Life goes on." Rubina couldn't help the anger interwoven through her words. She had a right to it after all—having earned it the hard way.

"Pearla, perhaps we should go," the redheaded woman said to Noah's bride. "I think it's safe to say the wedding is not going on as planned."

A tear fell down Pearla's cheek. Rubina would feel sorry for her, but she couldn't. She knew what it was like to have Noah's love. Jealousy turned her green with envy. Noah was only supposed to love her. For that alone, Rubina hated Pearla.

"You're right, Gemma." She nodded. "Can you take me home?"

Gemma nodded. "Of course." She looked over at Liam. "Are you going to stay, or…?"

Liam looked from Gemma to Noah, and then back to Rubina. He nodded. "I think I might be needed here. See Pearla home. I will call on you later when all of this"—he motioned between Rubina and Noah—"is settled."

"You should go, Liam," Rubina urged. "I think Noah and I can settle this between us without you overseeing anything."

"I'm staying," he said. His jaw tightened in determination.

"Suit yourself." Rubina shrugged.

She was mildly amused by the domesticity Liam showed Gemma. There was an intimacy there. He loved her, and perhaps they were already married. She never thought she'd see the day when Liam Marsden succumbed to love. He'd vowed to never marry. Well, wonders would never cease—even he could fall hopelessly for a woman.

"Ruby?" Noah approached her. "We should go home too. We can talk there."

"What, you don't want to air out our difficulties for the whole world?"

She didn't wish to make things easy for him. Nothing had been easy for her since Paolo kidnapped her three years ago. Rubina wanted him to feel every ounce of pain she experienced in his hands. He didn't know grief, but soon he would.

"Please," he begged.

It was a start. She wanted him on his knees prostrating himself before her. Even then she wasn't sure it would be enough. Her heart broke into a million shards when she found out he was planning on getting married again. Rubina wasn't sure if she'd ever be able to piece them together again. Her love for him was forever altered by his choice.

She needed some distance. Time to cry her heart

out without witnesses—after she got what she came for she would find someplace to lick her wounds. As much as she'd like to, she couldn't make Noah beg for anything, Rubina needed him to hate her.

"No." She shook her head. "I don't think I will go anywhere with you ever again."

He reeled back as if she'd slapped him. "Why?"

"I think it's pretty obvious."

"But it isn't." Noah took a step toward her. He raised a hand as if to touch her but let it drop to his side. "You're here. Alive. It's something I never believed possible."

"And yet you were about to take a bride and move on as if I'd never existed."

His face paled. "It's not like that, Ruby."

She tilted her head and studied him. Uncontrollable laughter spilled out of her lips. It was time to lay things down for Noah to understand. Rubina did not take this lightly. It was all too important for her to do what she came here for. As much as it pained her, it was time for Noah to look at her with the hatred she needed him to feel.

"It's exactly like that, Noah." She smiled at him. "So I'm going to do us both a favor and let you go."

"What?" he asked, confusion filling his eyes once again. "I don't want that."

Rubina had to be harsh. It was the only way to make him see her way was best.

"I want a divorce."

Noah flinched. "No."

"No?"

He shook his head. "Absolutely not. I won't give you one."

"Not even if I was unfaithful?"

His lips tightened at her words. Rubina had hit her mark dead on. It was the only way. She loved him, but he clearly didn't love only her anymore. As much as she believed Noah belonged to her, Rubina knew when to cut her losses and move on. She loved him enough to let him go.

Noah was only holding on because he believed in forever and he'd made her promises. If he'd believed she was still alive, he'd never have stopped looking for her. She wouldn't have found him about to marry another woman. Her Noah was honorable.

"You didn't—couldn't have."

"I'm sorry, Noah, dear." She patted his chest lightly and gazed up at him through hooded eyes. "I don't love you anymore."

He roared loud with denial. Oh, how fierce he looked, a lock of his dark hair falling over his forehead. Rubina resisted the urge to push it back in place.

"I don't believe you."

"Believe what you will." She shrugged. "But it's time to let go. This is good, no? You can marry your perfect fiancée and live happily as if I never existed."

"Stop. Just stop talking." He paced back and forth in front of the altar.

"Noah…"

"I said to be quiet," he seethed. His anger flashing within his eyes.

Rubina did as he asked and watched him in silence. He stopped suddenly and turned toward her. No longer was his gaze filled with shock. He'd overcome it all and had a new emotion ruling him. Pure rage. His cheeks were flushed a bright red. Noah clenched his fists at his sides as he stalked toward her. If he had less control, Rubina had no doubt he'd strike her.

"Why did you come back?" he asked.

"To set you free."

"No, I was already free."

"Were you?" She raised an eyebrow. "Or did I still haunt you even a little bit?"

He flinched. Her words hit another mark. She

knew Noah too well. Of course her death paid a toll on him. But still, he'd found another to love.

"Apparently I didn't do the same to you. You appear rather—healthy." He looked her up and down. "For someone presumed dead."

He had no idea what she went through. It'd been three weeks since her rescue. She'd had time to heal and gain a little weight on their passage from Italy to England.

"I've never felt better," she retorted.

He studied her. "A little too thin, but yes definitely glowing and content."

Noah knew her too. He'd notice that while she gained some weight, it had not been nearly enough. Her struggle to survive in order to make Paolo pay, it took everything inside her to get through it. She still had to make sure Paolo never hurt another soul again—soon he'd feel her wrath.

Another reason to let Noah go.

If Paolo believed she no longer wanted Noah, he'd leave her husband be. She had to protect him at all costs. Just because he moved on didn't mean she had. Rubina would always love Noah.

"I don't know. I think my figure is finally perfect." She ran her hands down her waist. "My gowns have never fit so well."

"You were perfect before." He paused. "You still are."

"Damian should be here soon with the divorce papers I had drawn up." She had to distract him before she threw herself at her husband. She loved Noah so much. It hurt to hurt him. "You'll sign them, yes?"

"I said no," he shouted. "I will never divorce you. If you didn't want me, you should have stayed dead."

It was Rubina's turn to flinch.

"I didn't mean that how it sounded."

"I'm sure you didn't," Rubina said softly.

Then Noah did the one thing she didn't expect from him. He lifted her up and threw her over his shoulder. Then with quick, purposeful strides he carried her out of the church. The guests still sitting in their pews watching the show—like predators stalking their prey. The gossip mills would be rolling with the scene by the end of the day.

"Put me down."

Liam called out, "I'll take care of things here, Noah. Go take care of your wife."

"I plan on it," he replied.

CHAPTER THREE

*R*ubina was alive.

Noah still couldn't wrap his head around it. She squirmed in his arms as he carried her out of the church. So full of life and energy and simply amazing. Having her with him had been his greatest wish, and now, by some miracle, it had been granted.

Let her go?

Not a chance in hell would he ever let her ago again. They might have a lot to work through, but suddenly he had a reason to fight. He'd fight anything and anyone—including Rubina herself—to have her with him again, forever.

"Noah, I said put me down."

"And I believe I already told you no."

He carried her all the way to his carriage. Noah opened the door and set her inside, climbing in after her. The carriage jerked forward as the driver flicked the reins, urging the horses to move. Rubina sat across from him, a mulish expression on her face.

She was so bloody lovely.

"Now, how about you start explaining to me where you've been for the past three years."

Rubina stayed silent. Her eyes shot daggers at him. Fine. She wanted to give him the silent treatment. He could work with that for now. Noah knew his wife. It was next to impossible for her to not say a word for long.

"How about I tell you what I've been doing for the past three years instead."

Nothing. She turned her head to look out the carriage window, attempting to ignore him. God, he loved her. He'd almost forgotten what it was like to have her around. She breathed life into him by just sharing the same space.

"When I heard your ship sank in a freak storm it felt like my heart was ripped out of my chest. I stayed drunk for days, weeks, hell, it might have been months."

Her jaw clenched. Good, at least she was listening.

"If not for Liam, I might have drank myself into an early grave. He took to staying with me for weeks on end. He dumped out every ounce of alcohol remaining on my estate. Then, he waited for me to start living again."

A small tear fell down her cheek. Noah took that as a good sign. If he kept talking, explaining, maybe she'd tell him what happened to her. Why she'd stayed gone for so long.

"You seem to be doing that rather well," she replied.

Noah smiled. He knew she couldn't stay silent.

"Looks can be rather deceiving. You know that."

Her gray eyes grew stormy as she studied him. "I do. A wedding is generally a damn good indicator you've moved on."

He had to find a way to make her understand why he'd decided to marry Pearla.

"Maybe on the outside looking in."

"It matters not." Rubina shook her head. "Once you sign the divorce papers we both can move on."

"I'm not saying this again." He glared at her. "There's not a chance in hell you will ever obtain my signature on those papers. Even if you did, it would take a lot for parliament to agree to grant the divorce. I won't even get into how much it would cost."

"I'm not worried about the money. It will be worth it to be free. Pay whatever is necessary. Take it out of my dowry." Rubina's face was devoid of emotion. "Just make it happen."

Why was she so eager to be free of him?

"Ruby, please, talk to me."

He tried to remain calm. Noah learned that lesson the hard way. When they met, he was reckless and so much in love he couldn't hold in his emotions for anything. They were all on the surface. His anger, love, frustrations—there was no reason to hold them back. Until one argument sent her fleeing away from him and he'd lost her. Now, she sat in front of him wanting to leave him again.

"There is nothing to discuss. Grant me the divorce I seek and we'll never need to see each other again."

"Is it really so bad to be with me?"

It hurt to ask, but he had to know. He still couldn't believe she was alive. Had she hidden from him all these years? Did he frighten her?

"I can't be around you."

The words were like a knife to his heart.

"Why?"

Rubina pursed her lips and stared him in the eyes. "I told you. I no longer love you."

Noah couldn't—wouldn't believe it. How could she have suddenly stopped loving him? Then he remembered, it hadn't been sudden. She'd been gone for three years. Maybe she never loved him at all.

"So you want me to believe you love someone else."

"Yes." She nodded.

Another jab right into the pain mass he called his heart. How much more could he take?

"Did you ever love me?"

"Maybe. I don't know. I was a foolish young girl rushing into marriage. What young person truly knows what is in their heart or what love really is."

Noah knew. He loved Rubina more than life. He still did.

Disgust filled him. He was such a bloody fool to keep holding on to her. She'd been his everything and, to her, he'd been nothing more than a passing fancy. Well, she'd made her bed, and she was bloody well going to lie in it.

"I will grant your divorce on one condition."

She studied him and asked, "I thought you were against it."

He had been. Noah didn't want to believe she'd

never loved him. He might be a fool, but even he could see through something if he looked at it long enough. Rubina didn't want him. Fine. He'd let her go, but not before she gave him something in return.

"I've had a few moments to assess the situation, and I can see a way for this to be mutually beneficial to us both."

She remained quiet for a few moments. "What are your conditions?"

"I will petition parliament for a divorce and pay all the hefty fees—out of my own pocket. I will even return the full amount of your dowry to you. You only have to agree to one small thing."

"That's a generous offer. What do I have to do in order for you to do all that?"

He smiled. Noah had her reeled in right where he needed her to be. She was interested enough to ask questions. Now he just needed her to agree to his demands.

"Give me an heir."

She gasped. "That's preposterous. You were about to get married. Get your new bride to give you a son."

"I was only marrying Pearla to have a child. I needed a wife for a legitimate heir." He paused and gave her a wicked grin. "Since I still have a wife, I don't see a reason to marry again. Spend a year with me. Bear my child, and only then will I do whatever is necessary to grant you your freedom."

"No"

He shrugged. "Fine. Then be content on being my wife until we both pass on from this world."

"Why are you being so difficult?"

Because he got his greatest wish. His one true love was alive. The only caveat was she appeared hate him. What was it people said? He should've been careful what he'd wished for because the reality was far from what he remembered. This was a cruel joke, but he intended to make the best of it. Liam had a point. It wasn't fair to marry Pearla when he knew he could never love her. Rubina could give him the heir he needed, and he could let her go. It seemed to be what she really wanted. After all, she'd stayed away from him for three years, letting him believe she died. She must despise him to do something so horrible. She only surfaced to gain her freedom to marry another man.

"I like to see it as a win-win situation. You get what you want, and I do too."

Life hardened him. Losing her destroyed him. She made him this way, and she would have to deal with those consequences. Earlier, he'd been drowning himself one final time in his own misery before his wedding. Now, he wondered why he'd bothered.

"You expect me to have a child. To leave and never see him again. What if it's a girl?" She frowned. "What would you tell them about where I am?"

"I suppose you'd better hope we accomplish our goal the first time." Noah shrugged. "As to where you were... I'd tell them you died."

She gasped and held her hand against her heart. "Even though I'd still be alive?"

"You're already dead to me, Rubina. Why should you be alive for our child?"

Harsh words, but Noah couldn't help the disgust filling him. For a brief moment, he'd been happy when he saw her standing in the church. He'd thought God had finally listened to his prayers and gave him back his beloved. Then she'd sat across from him and ripped his heart out over and over again.

She never really loved him.

"What happened to you?" she asked, softly. "This is not the Noah I remember."

"That man died when you did. It's best you acclimate yourself to the person you created when you ran away from me and faked your own death."

"I didn't do that."

"Run away from me or fake your own death?" He waved his hand. "Never mind, it doesn't matter. You made your choice and now you must deal with the consequences. Do you agree to my terms?"

"I can't abandon my own child." Her gaze pleaded with him. "Please, don't do this."

"If you ever want to see your new love again, you will agree to my terms. Or have you already started to share his bed? You're not already enceinte are you?" Noah glared at her. "I will not accept another man's bastard. As long as you are with me, you will be with no one else."

"I've not…" She gulped. " I lied earlier. I've only ever been with you."

He nodded. He wasn't surprised she would attempt a turnabout. "I will take your word. Whatever it's worth these days."

"I'm telling you the truth."

Noah wanted to believe her, but when his own wife didn't want him, it was hard to believe a word she said. She purposely ripped his heart out and made him believe she died. Why say she loved another unless she really did? Was she that cruel? How could he ever trust her again?

"So, do we have an agreement?" he asked.

Rubina turned away from him and stared out the carriage window again. It came to a halt, forcing her forward. She landed in his lap. He picked her up and set her firmly in his arms. The scent of honeysuckle drifted in his nose. His wife smelled exactly as he remembered her. He held back the urge to do what he needed. Noah desperately wanted to kiss her and feel her squirm with desire in his arms.

Rubina's eyes met his. Then, he just knew she'd had the same thoughts he did. His wife was not as unaffected by him as she let him believe. She may claim to love another man, but she still desired him. It was something he could work with. Maybe it could be enough to convince her to give in to his demands.

He pulled her close enough so their breaths mingled together. His hand cupped her breasts and rubbed his palm across it. Her nipples pebbled with the movement. Noah smiled wickedly. Before she could object, he captured her lips with his own. She gasped, giving him the opportunity to deepen the kiss. Her hands flew to his head grasping his hair and pulling him closer. Passion ignited between them, and Noah couldn't get close enough to her. Heat burned through him, and he felt himself harden beneath her.

Oh yes, his wife still wanted him.

He pulled back and looked at her swollen lips. Her eyes were pools of silver and her breathing ragged. Noah had done that to her. Made her forget the other man she claimed to love.

He flashed her a cocky grin. "I take that as a yes?"

Rubina nodded. "Fine. You win. One year." She started to pullback. "And then I will be gone."

"Not so fast, dear." He yanked her back into his arms. "I'm not letting you go so easily. We need to seal this deal once and for all in the only place we can."

"Where's that?" she asked.

He pushed the carriage door open and stepped out in front of his townhouse, not once letting go of her.

"In my bedroom, of course."

CHAPTER FOUR

*N*oah set Rubina down just in front of the door step but held on to her hand. It took every ounce of her self control to not yank it free and run. This plan of hers was not going at all how she had envisioned it. He was supposed to be disgusted and willingly give her a divorce. Her husband needed to do whatever it took to distance himself from her.

Now that she wasn't lost in his kiss, she was able to see reason once again. She couldn't stay with him and give him a child. If she did—she'd never leave. In truth, she never wanted to leave him. Until Paolo was taken care of, Noah would not be safe. The man had an unnatural obsession with her. There wasn't a doubt in her mind he'd murder Noah in truth at the first opportunity. Paolo had to believe Noah didn't want her and that she'd moved on to someone else.

"Noah." Rubina set her free hand on his chest and looked up at him. "This isn't a good idea."

He glared down at her. His chocolate brown eyes filled with anger. "Too late. You've already agreed."

He pushed open the door and led her inside their home. It was exactly as she'd remembered it. Noah must not have changed a thing. A lump of emotion welled up inside of her. If only things were different...

"Your Grace..." Simmons stopped short and looked between the two of them. It took a lot to ruffle the proper butler and the return of the duke's wife was a good excuse if ever there was one. He recovered quickly and bowed before them both. "Welcome home."

"Hello, Simmons," Rubina greeted him. "I assume my chamber is prepared."

Simmons blinked, but showed no outward emotion. "Of course, Your Grace."

He didn't mention it had been prepared for a new duchess. That would have been unseemly. Rubina didn't care though. It gave her an avenue for escape. Noah wanted too much from her. Another time and another place she'd have willingly given it to him.

"Excellent. It's been a long day. I think I'll rest for a while. Could you have something light sent up to me? I don't much feel like company."

"I'll let one of the maids know." He nodded and headed down the hall.

Rubina walked toward the stairs, but was jerked back suddenly by Noah.

"Not so fast, dear." A wicked smile greeted her.

"We can talk later." Rubina stared into his eyes. "We have plenty of time to get reacquainted."

He nodded. "You're right."

Relief flooded through her. Maybe he was starting to rethink his demands. Rubina certainly hoped so. She didn't know if she could leave if she spent even one second in her husband's bed. This would give her the time necessary to escape.

"I'm glad you're finally being reasonable."

"Reason has nothing to do with my decision. There are a few matters I need to take care of. We will continue where we left off."

Rubina bit her lip. Part of her was irritated he was running off. This was what she wanted though. Right? In order to keep Noah safe.

"Don't worry about me. I'll be fine on my own."

He smiled, but it didn't reach his eyes. "I didn't intend to. You, my dear, can get by where others fear to tread. I have no doubt you'll come out of anything completely intact."

That hurt. A lot. But Rubina wasn't going to let him know how wrong he was. She was not the same woman he married years ago. She'd been to hell and back. There might not be any physical scars, but the ones deep inside flared up with pain at the slightest provocation.

"That's correct. I'm a survivor. I won't make any apologies for it."

And she wouldn't. She made it to the other side to invoke her revenge. Rubina was patient, and her tormentor would know true pain when she was done with him.

"I didn't ask you to." He raised an eyebrow as he stared down at her. "A little touchy aren't you?"

Damn it. She'd not wanted to give him a reason to question her.

"Not at all. Just reminding you of who I am now."

The muscles in his jaw clenched at her words. "There's not any chance of that happening. Trust me I will never forget how little you care for me. It's a life lesson I didn't think I'd ever live through."

"I'm glad we understand each other."

"Oh, I am all too aware of who you are. A part of me wonders if I never fully saw you. Did you pretend to love me? Was the idea of being a duchess such a grand idea that you pretended to be someone you're not?"

"I never pretended with you."

At least not then. Now, she'd be whoever he needed her to be. As long as it made him send her in the opposite direction. Loving Noah was her greatest joy and her deepest fear. If she'd not caught the attention of a mad man everything would be so different. Perhaps she'd have a child already and they'd still be so blissfully happy. Unfortunately, wishing didn't make it so. They were very far from ever having that again. It had all been ruined by her impetuous decision to flee to Italy to visit her family. She couldn't take back that decision, as much as she'd like to. The life she'd begun with Noah wasn't to be. Soon he'd be free to marry the young woman he'd been set to marry. With her, he could have the family he desired. She'd see it happen.

"I don't believe you."

Rubina wanted to defend herself, but she couldn't. This was good. He doubted her, and that would make it easier for him to set her aside. To grant her divorce, setting them both free. She could pursue Paolo with a clear conscience knowing Noah was safe.

"It matters not. The past is where it belongs. It's best not to rehash something that cannot be changed."

"Truer words have never been spoken." He glared at her. "Don't leave this house, Rubina. I will find you, and you'll not like it when I do."

He spun on his heels and headed in the opposite direction of her. She'd landed a blow to his pride. Noah had always had an abundant amount, and now Rubina had wounded it. It was for the best. She couldn't let him love her anymore. Even if she would always love him.

Rubina sighed. She had to get out of the house and away from Noah despite his warning. Coming home with him had been a huge mistake. It was something she should not have allowed to happen. Paolo had spies everywhere. If he knew she'd become reacquainted with her husband, he could already be making plans to kill him.

She headed to the front door and pulled it open wide. Standing with her hand in mid-knock was the brazen red-head from the wedding.

"Oh, pardon me. I was about to…"

"Knock on the door?" Rubina raised an eyebrow. "That was obvious. How can I help you?"

Her eyebrows scrunched up in puzzlement. "Why were you answering the door? Where's Simmons?"

Rubina glared down at her. Insipid creature. Why did she feel she had a right to question her? What was her involvement with her husband? "This is my home."

"Could have fooled me." She pushed her way inside. "Seeing as you left it several years ago without a second thought."

Rubina saw red. She did not like this woman.

"You have no idea what I've been through."

"Right. I don't know if I care either." She waved her hand dismissively. "I didn't come here to see you regardless. I need to talk to Noah."

She was on a first name basis with her husband? Rubina didn't like that one bit. The jealousy bug hit her hard. When she saw him ready to marry the blonde she'd dismissed it. She didn't realize it until that moment, but he seemed—detached during the ceremony. This woman seemed different somehow.

"He's busy."

"Oh?" She studied Rubina. "With what?"

"Business, I presume."

It killed her to admit that. She had no idea what Noah was taking care of.

"I find it rather odd that his wife comes back

from the dead, and he's abandoned her to take care of business."

If it had been a true reunion Noah wouldn't have left her for any reason. She'd goaded him until he'd stormed off. Rubina wouldn't let this woman know that.

"I'm sure it has something to do with dissolving the wedding that didn't happen. Since I'm alive and well, he can't very well wed another woman."

She nodded. "That's why I'm here actually. Is he in his study?"

The odious woman started to head toward Noah's study. Rubina couldn't let her disturb him. She'd finally got him to leave her in peace. Escape would become rather impossible if he came back out. This intruder had to leave—and soon. Otherwise, she'd have a hard time meeting up with Damian. They had a rendezvous point, and it would soon be well past their scheduled time.

"He doesn't want to be disturbed." Rubina grabbed her arm to stop her. "Maybe if you came back at another time."

She shook her head. "No, this can't wait."

"Listen…" What was her name anyway. They'd said at the church. Oh hell, it didn't matter. She needed to leave.

"Gemma, or Lady Marsden for you. I don't know that we'll be close enough to use first names."

"Fine, you can address me as Your Grace."

An evil smile formed on Gemma's face. "That's fine, Your Grace. Now get your bloody hand off of me so I can go talk to Noah."

"I can't do that, Lady Marsden." She clenched her teeth together.

Gemma brought her hand up on top of Rubina's and threaded her fingers into her. While she smiled sweetly, she yanked Rubina's hand back and twisted her wrist.

"Ouch! Was that really necessary?"

"I don't like to have anyone touching me that I didn't invite to do so."

Rubina glared. "You could have asked me to let go."

She raised an eyebrow. "Would you have?"

Probably not, but she didn't know that.

"I'm starting to see why Liam was drawn to you."

"Thanks." She frowned. "I think."

"It wasn't a compliment."

Rubina never did understand why Noah and Liam remained such good friends. They came from different worlds. Yes, they were both sons of noblemen, but Noah lived a life of isolation where Liam was encased in a loving family. Both were strong, reliable, and stubborn. Rubina believed that was why her husband was drawn to Liam's family. Being around them helped him get over the losses he had been dealt as a boy. They gave him something he craved. Liam helped him in so many ways.

He kept to himself and didn't encourage social interactions. Liam thrived and floated through society, not giving it a care. It came much easier for him. His wife was full of fire and life—a perfect fit for Liam. Rubina wished she'd been around to see their courtship. It must have been fascinating to watch. In another lifetime, maybe they could have been friends. She had a new respect for the woman.

"I will choose to take it as one regardless."

"What is going on here?"

Rubina gazed up into Noah's eyes. "We have a visitor."

"I can see that." He frowned. "Why are you here, Gemma?"

She smiled, reassuringly. "Do you have a moment to talk?" She looked over at Rubina. "In private?"

He nodded. "I always have time for you. Please come to my study."

Noah held his hand out, gesturing the way, letting Gemma walk before him.

He turned to head back in the direction he'd just come from. Noah stopped and pivoted toward Rubina. "Remember what I said earlier." His voice was harsh. "Don't make me come find you."

Gemma stopped and stared between them. She shook her head. Sadness filled her lovely green eyes.

Ruby didn't want her pity.

"Go. Have your visit." She smiled sweetly. "When you're done, by all means, please come find me. I promise you it will be something you'll never forget."

Instead of waiting for his reply, she went up the stairs with every ounce of pride she owned flowing through her. She held her head high and took each step with the poise and grace of a princess on her way to greet her subjects. No one would ever pity Rubina.

From the moment she got free until she'd made herself a promise, never again would she be a victim. She'd die a thousand deaths before she let anyone see her as weak again.

Especially Noah and Gemma Marsden.

Nothing would get her to admit how much it hurt to watch her husband dismiss her so easily. He barely gave her a second thought. Everything should have been so different. A tear traveled down her cheek. She quickly wiped it away. There wasn't time to give into the pain. This was the plan. It had to be this way.

Noah, the only man she would ever love, must always come first.

Only then would revenge be hers.

CHAPTER FIVE

*N*oah followed Gemma into his study. He held out a chair for her and then sat behind his desk.

"What can I do for you?"

Gemma took a deep breath and studied him in silence for several seconds. "First, tell me how you're doing."

How did he answer that question? His wife was alive. Something he'd dreamed of happening but never dared wish for. Good thing he hadn't because it was less than ideal.

"Did Liam send you over to check on me?"

Gemma shook her head. "No, of course not...I mean, not that he isn't probably concerned, but I haven't spoken to him since I left the church with Pearla."

"I see."

Noah stared off in space. The church—what a disaster that turned out to be. When he turned to see Rubina walking down the aisle… He stopped breathing for a second, sure he'd been seeing some apparition sent to play tricks on him. Then reality came crashing in, and it was all too real. Rubina was not only alive, but she claimed to no longer love him.

"Don't think I didn't notice how you failed to answer my question." Gemma smiled. "Nice try, but I'm not leaving until I am sure you're doing all right."

Noah sighed. "How do you think I'm doing?"

She raised an eyebrow. "I wouldn't presume to know. But if I were forced to guess, I'd say you're not doing well at all. Something isn't right because I'd have thought you'd be ecstatic to have your wife back."

"Under normal circumstances I would be." He ran his hand through his hair. "Let's be honest, nothing is normal about this situation. I can't make sense of any of it."

Gemma nodded. "I expect that is the only thing normal about this situation."

"I need a drink."

Noah stood and grabbed the nearly empty brandy decanter near his desk. That's right. He'd drank quite a bit of it in the morning before his wedding. Drinking hadn't helped that situation any more than it would help the one he currently found himself in. There was nothing that would help it.

Rubina was alive.

Maybe if he said it enough he'd truly believe it. The problem was she wasn't anything like he remembered. Oh, she was still as beautiful as the day he met her, but her eyes told a different story. She was harder and less forgiving. The loving woman he married didn't look back at him. Instead, a stranger had taken her place.

He set the decanter back down, rethinking his idea for a drink.

"Good choice," Gemma said.

"I feel like my whole world tipped upside down in the matter of minutes."

"Because it has."

"Drinking isn't going to make that right." He shook his head. "It will probably make it inherently worse."

She nodded. "Probably a good assumption."

Noah jerked his head around and asked, "How is Pearla doing?"

Gemma sighed. "That's why I'm here. She asked me to return this to you."

She set a ring down on his desk. It was an alabaster pearl flanked by brilliant diamonds. He'd purchased it for her specifically.

"No. I meant that for her. Give it back."

"I'm afraid I can't do that."

"Why the hell not?"

Noah clenched his fists at his side as anger seized his heart. Why couldn't anything go right in his life? Ever since his parents died, his whole existence was nothing but loneliness. If not for Liam and his family, he'd probably never go out and socialize. Everyone left him eventually. He felt...unlovable.

"Pearl has decided she can't stay in England." Gemma frowned. "She believes the stigma of what happened at the church makes her...undesirable."

"That's ridiculous." Noah glared at Gemma. "It's not her fault my wife pretended to be dead for years."

She cleared her throat. "She said to tell you she doesn't blame you for any of it. If you'd known Rubina was alive, you'd never have put her in that situation."

"Of course not. I'd have hunted her down and brought her home."

At least long enough to obtain his heir. Which he fully intended to get from her before she disappeared again. She may not love him anymore, but she owed him.

"Yes. As I was saying, she thinks you are very honorable and deserve far more than what's been dealt you." She took a breath. "Which is why she can't keep the ring. She says it's not fair to keep a token of your affection when she knows you are very much in love with your wife. She doesn't want anything to remind her of what could have been."

Noah's eyes whipped upward. As he stared into Gemma's, he asked, "Come again?"

"She believed herself to be in love with you. This wasn't a business deal for her."

Noah scrubbed his hands over his face. Could this day get any worse? He'd thought she knew—understood—he was incapable of loving anyone else. Rubina took it all with her when she died—no, she still had it. She may be a deceptive witch, but he still loved the illusion.

"I'm so sorry. I didn't know…"

"Don't feel guilty. She wouldn't want you to." Gemma reached across the desk and placed her hand on his arm. "It was her choice. One she thought she could live with. Now it's time for her to accept a different path. Just as you must. Your wife is alive and upstairs waiting to start your lives together again."

"No, she isn't." Noah frowned. "She can't wait to be rid of me."

"No? Why would she come back if she doesn't want to be with you? There must be some other explanation. I don't believe for a minute she doesn't still love you."

"You're wrong." Noah swept his arms across his desk, knocking everything to the floor. The brandy glass from earlier shattered on impact. "She wants a divorce. Ruby stated her wishes clearly before the entire guest list at my failed wedding."

He stood and started to pace. Noah turned to look at her and stopped in place.

Gemma's face had lost all color.

From the look on her face, he'd frightened her. He'd make it up to her later. When he got his feelings under control.

"There must be some mistake," Gemma said.

Noah's hand shook as he covered his face. That's what he kept telling himself. It was all a grievous mistake. Rubina didn't love him anymore. He'd heard wrong. It was all some bizarre nightmare he'd wake up from at any moment.

"I'm afraid not."

"I don't understand."

He shook his head and fought tears. Men didn't cry. Noah wanted to give in, but he wouldn't, not with Gemma still in the room. "That makes two of us."

"Why is she still here if she wants a divorce?"

A bark of laughter escaped his mouth. "Because I made a deal with her."

Gemma stood up and approached him. "What did you do?"

He'd bargained with one of the devil's servants. It was the only thing he could think to do when she'd cornered him with her insane request. There was no way parliament was going to grant him a divorce. No matter how much he paid them to get out of it. There was only way to end a marriage—one of them had to die.

They were stuck together whether she liked it or not.

"I agreed to her terms if she agreed to mine."

"What did you ask for?"

Noah looked down at her and replied, "I asked for a child."

"Oh, Noah."

Sadness filled her eyes. He didn't like the way she

was staring at him. Gemma meant well, but she didn't know what it was like to live inside his skin. To know love and then have it ripped from him— nothing hurt more than that. Even though both his parents died while he was a child, this was so much more painful. His heart was ripped to shreds with no hope of being repaired.

"Don't look at me like that."

"I'm sorry."

He frowned. "What for? You didn't do it. You've always been a good friend to me. Without you and Liam I'd be alone."

At least he wouldn't inflict himself upon Pearla. She may think she loved him, but in time, she'd probably get over that. She escaped a bad fate by escaping marriage to him. He was a bad bet.

"You're a good friend too. Don't sell yourself short." She stepped up to him and wrapped her arms around his waist, hugging him. Her head lay upon his chest. "Rubina doesn't know what she's missing by not staying with you forever. It's her loss, not yours."

"Then why does it feel like I've lost a piece of myself?" He wrapped his arms around her, returning the hug. "Everything I thought was up is down and vice versa."

She took a step back. A lone tear fell down her cheek. He reached up and wiped it away. "It won't always be that way. One day you'll wake up and realize you're going to be just fine. The ache that takes over your heart won't be quite as painful and breathing will come a little easier. It only feels so devastating because it's all fresh and new."

"How do you know?"

"I was you once. When I first told Liam I loved him he practically ran in the other direction. It wasn't a grand love story like you and Rubina—but it was very real to me. It took a while for me to move on with my life. It helps to have something else to focus on."

He shook his head. "Liam was an ass."

She smiled. "He was then, yes. And he certainly can be still, but I love him regardless."

Noah nodded. "He's lucky."

"Rubina is too." She placed a hand on his arm. "She will realize it eventually. I'm sure she has reasons for what she's doing."

"She does. She claims to love another and wants to be free to be with them."

She shook her head. "She's lying."

"I don't think she is."

Gemma smiled. "I'm willing to bet she still loves

you very much. You should ask her about her time apart from you. There's something she's not telling you."

Noah didn't think there was. He didn't really want to listen to tales of her new love. It would hurt too much. No, it was much better not knowing all the gory details. He was afraid of what they were and what they would tell him about his wife. All of his illusions had already been shattered. Why make it even more difficult that it already was? Maybe after he calmed down he'd demand answers. For the moment, he was all right without them.

"I'd rather not know."

"That's your choice to make, but Noah..." He looked down at her. "She does still love you. You can count on it."

"How could you possibly know that?"

She smiled. "Because you didn't see how she looked at you when you weren't looking."

He shook his head. "That means nothing. So what if she still desires me? That does not equate love by any means."

It didn't. Rubina may still own his heart, but she took hers back. She wanted to give it completely to another man. Noah couldn't stomach the idea.

"It's not the same thing."

"No. Lust burns out a lot faster. Love is supposed to be forever."

"I wouldn't know." She shook her head. "I do know what a woman in love looks like, and your wife never stopped loving you."

She held up her hand when he started to speak, stopping him.

"Let me finish. You can do what you want with that information, but I think if you try hard enough, in time, she'll admit the truth to you."

"I don't know." He frowned.

"I do." She smiled. "Take this little bit of advice. Don't toss what you had aside. Try to see things from her point of view. Maybe dig a little deeper so you can see things from her side. Don't throw your marriage away without at least trying."

Noah sighed. "I'm not making any promises."

"I'm not asking you to," she said. "Now, I need to get home to my husband. If you need someone to talk to, come see me or Liam. We'll always be here for you."

Gemma headed toward the door to leave.

"Wait," he called out to her.

"Yes?"

"You never did say where Pearla was going."

She smiled. "I don't know. She didn't want me to slip and tell you."

Great. Women seemed to be in a hurry to run away from him, and they didn't want him to be able to track them down. Gemma meant well, but he didn't think she saw things as they were. Rubina would give him a child. That's all he needed from her. Then she could run away and never come back. Noah would find a way to be content with that.

Even if he had to become even more closed off than he already was.

CHAPTER SIX

*R*ubina rushed through Piccadilly and headed toward The Albany. Damian had a set of rooms there. It was a bachelor residence he kept so he had his own place when he visited London. He'd acquired them when Rubina married Noah. Her brother hadn't wanted to intrude on her new marriage, but he still wanted to be able to visit her. She didn't know why he'd kept them upon her supposed death, but the rooms would be their meeting point now. Luckily, they allowed her entrance. There was a time when a woman hadn't been allowed to even enter the prestigious bachelor residence.

Rubina looked over her shoulder. A niggling

feeling someone was watching her crawled over her skin. She didn't know where it came from, but she couldn't shake the sensation. No one seemed to be around. Still, she'd have to be careful. Just because she couldn't see anyone didn't mean they weren't there.

Rubina shook it off and lifted her skirts, rushing toward the entrance of The Albany. She headed straight to Damian's set of rooms and knocked on the door. It flew open after a few seconds. Damian looked up and down the hall and yanked her inside.

"You're late."

Rubina peeled off her gloves and tossed them on a nearby table. "I know. It couldn't be helped." She strolled over to a chaise and sat, letting out the breath she'd not realized she'd been holding. "Do you have news?"

He nodded. "Nothing specific. Just a rumbling."

"Tell me."

"In all due time." Damian walked to a nearby window and peered outside. "What happened with Noah?"

"He's being difficult."

Damian let the curtain slide closed. He laughed. "What did you expect?"

Rubina frowned. "I'd hoped he would be so disgusted with me he wouldn't question my request."

Damian frowned. "He loves you, Rue. When you died—when he thought you were gone—he shattered. I can't imagine how it must have been for him to see you alive in front of him. It must have been quite a shock."

Rubina looked away. Her brother had no idea how hard it was to stick to the plan when she saw Noah in the church. The look on his face… It tore her apart. But in order for Noah to live, she had to break him even more.

"Indeed."

"So why did it take you so long to get back here?"

Rubina sighed. "Noah absconded with me and took me home."

"That had to be difficult." He shook his head and laughed again. "Though I'm not at all surprised he did. I'd have done the same."

"I'm sure you would." She bit her lip. "He's not going to go along with the divorce so easily—he wants more than I can give him."

She couldn't help wanting to give in to his demands. To make love with her husband and create a child together… Rubina would give anything to have it all. Fate had other ideas for what she could have though.

"So what does he require to see the divorce through."

She waved a hand. "It matters not. I can't give it to him. We'll have to find another way."

"There is no other way. We already discussed this in length. Paolo has to believe you've severed all ties, or else he will go after Noah."

"I know," she exclaimed. "If only we could put an end to this…"

The crafty bastard was in hiding. They couldn't locate him anywhere. When Arturo had brought her to Damian, he hadn't known why Paolo couldn't be found. He was on a secret mission that no one had all the details for. Rubina was partially glad he'd disappeared. It made her rescue possible. The downside was no one knew exactly where he was—which put Noah in danger.

"My sources all point to London. He has to be here." Damian frowned. "If he isn't he will be soon."

"That's what I'm afraid of." Rubina shook her head. "Why couldn't he be on the other side of the world and far away from my husband?" She sighed. "I think I was followed here."

"Did you see anyone?" He skimmed the curtains with his hands and looked outside again. "We can't be too careful with your safety. Perhaps I should accompany you when you leave."

"It was more of a sensation of being watched." She didn't need Damian to go into protector mode. Rubina suffocated enough under Paolo's control. "Let the evil bastard make his move. It will give me the opportunity to finish this. Noah will come around and grant me a divorce. It's his only option. For now I will take up residence in the townhouse we've rented for my stay in London."

"Noah is the key to all of this. I can feel it in my gut." Damian paced around the room. "I think you need to go back."

"What?" Her eyes widened in shock. "If I go back, he'll never let me out of his sight again. I'm lucky to have gotten away without him following me."

"How did you manage that?"

Rubina hadn't wanted to leave. If she'd been given a choice, she'd never leave her husband again. Especially with a beautiful woman keeping him company. She gritted her teeth and clenched her hands into tight fists when he left her alone to speak to Gemma in private. The only way she had been able to allow the slight was to remind herself over and over again the other woman was married to Liam Marsden. The one thing she knew for certain was Liam would never stand for his wife to stray—especially with his best friend. He was no cuckold.

"He had a visitor. I took advantage and slipped out while he was occupied."

Damian's eyebrow rose. "I'm surprised he let you out of his sight. Noah doesn't seem like the type to allow you to take advantage of a situation."

He was correct. Under normal circumstances Noah wouldn't have been so easily duped. Her husband had his whole world turned upside down in a short time. He wasn't at his best—which Rubina took advantage of. When he had time to stop and think, he'd know exactly where she could be found. He'd warned her after all. Which meant she'd have to wrap up her meeting with Damian soon and make herself scarce...

"He isn't. It's been a hard day—I expect he'll be by soon in a full fury."

"Really?" He smiled. "I suppose you're correct. I look forward to the visit. Now go home to your husband."

"No. You know I can't."

"I know you want to protect Noah, but I think the time for that has passed."

"You don't know that for certain."

Damian folded his arms across his chest and stared down at her. "I do."

"How?"

He crossed the room and pulled out a slip of paper from a drawer. Damian looked back at her and frowned, then walked to her side. "I received this coded message just before you arrived. Take a look at it."

Rubina opened the folded note and scanned the contents. "Arturo can verify this?"

Damian nodded. "We may not have located Paolo, but we have discovered his mission."

She shot to her feet and paced the room. Rubina didn't say a word for several minutes. Her mind whirled at what Arturo had discovered. How could Noah have been so reckless? He'd unwittingly put himself in far graver danger than she'd realized. There was no protecting him with distance now. She'd have to stay. Her heart leapt with joy at the prospect. Leaving him had never been her wish—but how much could she tell him.

Damian nodded. "Noah invested in some orchards along the coast of Sicily near Palermo. If I were to hazard a guess, it was something to remind him of you and where he met you."

"Oh hell…"

"The Mafioso doesn't like usurpers. They want control of that property. Paolo is all too glad to deal with it, knowing how important he is to you. He'd gladly end Noah's life."

"I'm too late." She threw up her hands. "I broke him even further for nothing."

Tears fell from her eyes. She wiped them away. They wouldn't help the situation. A new plan had to be formed. Noah would not die because of his ties to her and her family.

"So what am I to do now?"

Damian pulled her into his arms. He hugged her tight. "Don't worry, Rue. I won't let them kill Noah. Paolo will pay for what he's done to you and our family."

Rubina pulled back and steeled herself for their next move. "He will pay. I'll gladly be the one to end his life. Paolo is an evil man and shouldn't be allowed to inflict any more pain on another soul."

"I can't let you do that. You already have too much to deal with." He shook his head. "First and foremost, you need to go home to your husband. Watch everyone around him. Anyone and everyone is suspect. Paolo could take the opportunity to instill someone in Noah's house to spy on him. We can't take a chance someone might start feeding him crucial information. You need to be there to prevent any potential danger to your husband."

Rubina nodded. "You're right. Of course, he would try to plant a spy there. Paolo is nothing if not efficient."

And smart. Rubina intended to be smarter. She would have to be to defeat him.

"When I know more, I'll come by."

"What am I to tell Noah?"

Damian shrugged. "Tell him you went for a walk. Whatever you can to distract him. I'm not so sure it's a good idea he knows everything yet. He can be —hardheaded."

Rubina snorted. Damian didn't have to tell her how stubborn her husband could be. She knew all too well how he could dig his heels in when a notion came over him. In those times, up was down and vise versa. No one could persuade him when he got an idea about something.

"At some point we will have to tell him everything."

Damian nodded. "I know. Just not yet. Play along with whatever he wants for now. It shouldn't be much longer, and then you can unburden yourself."

The truth shall set her free...

Hopefully Noah wouldn't hate her too much when that time came.

"All right." She picked up her gloves off the table and slid them back on. "I'll return to Noah. I won't say anything for now. But Damian..." She stared him in the eyes. "Find Paolo. End this. I don't know how long I can keep up this pretense without breaking."

"I am working as hard and as fast as I can." He ran his hands through his chestnut hair. His silver eyes filled with worry. "There are only so many places he could be, and I will find him."

Rubina nodded. "I hope so."

A thunderous boom filled the room. It echoed throughout the entire residence. The earsplitting racket repeated over and over again. They both stopped and turned toward the entrance. A very unhappy person appeared to be knocking on Damian's door. There really could only be one person who would come by and hit his door with such force.

Noah had come looking for her.

He'd promised he would find her, after all. Where else would she have gone but to her brother. Her husband knew her better than he realized. She might be playing a game of illusions with him—making him doubt her—but at her core she hadn't changed. Rubina always ran to Damian for help. The only exception was Noah. When she met him and fallen in love, that dynamic changed slightly. She'd run to her husband first—unless her problem was about him.

"I think it's safe to say your husband is here."

Rubina glared at him. "Oh?" Sarcasm filled her voice. "What was your first clue?"

Another deafening boom filled the room.

Damian laughed. "I suppose I should let him in before he breaks down the door."

Her brother headed toward the door. He took his time. No reason to rush or anything. Noah was just about to do some serious damage to the entrance to his rooms. Why ever wouldn't he hurry to let him in? Rubina sometimes thought her brother had a death wish.

He eased the door open and greeted her husband. "Noah, how good to see you? What can I help you with?"

Noah raised an eyebrow in derision. "Don't treat me like an idiot. Give me my wife. Now."

Damian opened the door all the way allowing Noah to see Rubina.

Noah's smile was so full of wickedness it her caused her heart to speed up. She raised her hand across her chest and her mouth fell open in anticipation.

Oh my…

"Hello, dear. I told you I'd come for you."

CHAPTER SEVEN

"I wasn't exactly hiding." Rubina shrugged. "If you'd waited a little bit longer, I'd have returned home all on my own."

Noah stalked toward Rubina. When he'd discovered her missing, his vision went red. How dare she run off again. After what happened the last time...

He shook the image from his mind. She was alive. Something he had to constantly remind himself of. What had happened before was an elaborate ruse. He had no idea what her end game was, but he intended to find out. It was time for him to face the truth. He wanted answers, and he intended to make her start to doling them out. At least she'd been easy to find. Unlike before...

Of course she'd run to her brother. Damian had

always been the one person she'd turn to when she was mad at him. It was the first place he thought to look—even though he'd not been certain Damian was in London. But he was—where else would he be? How much did her brother know, and when did he find out? Noah wasn't happy with either one of them, and he planned on letting them both feel every ounce of his rage.

He raised an eyebrow. "I somehow doubt the validity of your statement."

"It's true." Damian jumped in. "Rue was just about to leave."

Noah jerked his head in his brother-in-law's direction. "How long have you known she was alive?" He seethed.

"Not as long as your look implies."

He tilted his head, crossed his arms, and studied Damian. "I'm willing to bet it's still longer than I've known. Tell me what you know."

Damian shrugged. "Not a whole lot. Rue found me near Palermo. One of my men showed her where to find me. I was shocked to see her alive."

Noah bet he was. Damian wasn't telling him everything. No doubt that little bit information was the truth—but he knew him well. There were details he was purposely holding back. In time, Noah would have them all. For now, he'd settle for dragging his wayward wife home where she belonged.

She owed him far more than her brother did. It was Rubina who had betrayed their love.

"Since you were leaving, my dear,"—he turned toward her—"I will escort you home."

Rubina smiled. "Why of course. Give me a moment to say goodbye to my brother."

She sashayed over to Damian and hugged him tight. "I will see you again soon, yes?"

"I promise."

She stepped out of Damian's arms and walked over to Noah. She looped her arm in his, tilted her head, and studied him through her lashes. "I believe you were taking me home…"

Her lips tilted into an enticing smile. It was an invitation Noah could not mistake. His wife intended to seduce him. He hardened at the thought. What game was she playing now?

He choked back the lump in his throat. Rubina would not get the best of him. It was time to take control and play things the way he wanted.

"Damian." He tore his gaze from his wife's plump lips. "I will speak to you later about this whole ordeal. I want more details. For now, we are leaving."

Damian nodded. "Absolutely. I will stop by and

speak with you in a few days. I'm sure you have many questions." His gaze landed on Rubina's and held it for several seconds—something unsaid passing between them.

Noah didn't know what they were hiding, but he would find out. It disgusted and irritated him that they went to such lengths to hold back the truth.

"I look forward to your visit. When you come by, make sure to leave some time for me." Rubina pouted prettily at her brother.

"I already said I'd visit you, Rue." He grinned. "How many promises do I need to make?"

"As many as I require." She flashed him a gamine smile.

"Enough. It's time to depart," Noah said roughly. This nonsense must come to an end.

"Goodbye, Damian." Rubina waved as Noah escorted her out of the room.

They walked outside to his awaiting carriage. His ducal crest emblazoned upon the door. He gritted his teeth so he didn't give her any more biting replies. She was fast driving him insane—though not in the way he wanted.

His every dream had come true when she boldly strolled down the church aisle, interrupting his wedding. Unfortunately, it fast turned into his worst nightmare. What difference did it make if his wife lived when she clearly despised him? What other reason would she have for staying away from him for so long? Well, she was in for a rude awakening. She wouldn't be able to get rid of him as easily as she wanted.

He helped her inside the carriage and joined her, sitting across from her. She looked out the window, apparently refusing to meet his gaze.

"Don't worry. We will be home soon enough."

She whipped her head to meet his gaze. Fury shot out of her eyes. Her fists clenched in her lap, but she quickly eased them into a relaxed state. "I wasn't worried about arriving home."

"No?" he asked, studying her beautiful face. "What could you possibly be fretting over?"

"It doesn't matter." She brushed it aside with the wave of her hand. "Nothing but trivial concerns. It isn't anything you need to bother yourself with."

"If it concerns you, it does me as well. Tell me what is on your mind."

Rubina bit her lip and looked back out the window. "It's just I don't have anything to wear."

Of course. His fashion conscious wife would be concerned about her lack of wardrobe. "If you wanted to purchase new gowns, all you had to do was ask. No reason to pout in silence."

Her smile brightened. "You were always so generous with me. Can we go to Madame Roussard's now?"

Noah frowned. "It's getting rather late in the day…"

"Please," she begged prettily. "I do so need some new gowns. If I'm to stay in England, I will need them to go out in society. The world needs to know your wife has returned."

"I know… but—"

"You don't want them doubting our child is yours do you?" She raised an eyebrow. "We must give them a united front, and show them how very much in love we still are."

"So you want me to lie?"

She tilted her head and studied him. "You're saying you no longer love me?"

Noah clenched his jaw as her words hit him where it hurt. She spoke the truth. He never stopped loving her, but he refused to admit it to her. He'd be damned before he gave her the satisfaction.

"Why don't you tell me why you really want new gowns, Ruby?" He leaned back against the of the seat, acting as relaxed as he possibly could.

"I already told you…"

He held up a hand. "Quit playing your silly games and tell me the truth."

She sighed. "I don't have but the gown I'm wearing and the one in my valise. I haven't gotten any new gowns since I left England three years ago. I've had to make do with a couple second-hand gowns."

Noah frowned. She was telling the truth. He could see it in her eyes. It didn't make any sense to him. If she'd been so destitute, why had she stayed away? He would have gladly bought her anything she wanted. Rubina had been his everything, and there was nothing he wouldn't have done for her. Did she really need to get away from him that bad? To live without any of the amenities she'd been used to?

"Why this pretense?"

"I don't know what your mean?" She frowned. "I am telling you the truth."

He believed her. That didn't mean he understood any of it.

"No." He shook his head. "With Damian and your father. Why not tell them you were alive? If you didn't want to be with me, they would have supported you. What were you thinking, Ruby?"

"I couldn't." She returned her gaze to the window.

"Bloody hell. Why not?"

"So, are we going to go to Madam Roussard's?"

She didn't meet his eyes. His wife didn't even bother to answer his question. Instead, she changed the subject. He could respect that a little bit. It was evasion at its best. He'd deflected her question about loving her just as easily. What a pair the two of them made.

"No, we are not going to the dress shop today."

Finally, she turned to look at him. Her silver eyes reflected sadness. "You never were cruel Noah. What happened to you?"

"My wife died."

She tilted her head. "But I am very much alive."

"You're not my wife." He stared her in the eyes. "You're an imposter living inside her body. The Rubina Leone I married loved me and would never have put me through the hell you have."

Rubina gasped. Her hand flew to her chest. Her gaze held resignation. "I deserve that."

She deserved so much more than mere words could inflict upon her. Noah held back all the anger building up inside of him. This wasn't the time nor the place to unleash it all on her. They would be home soon enough. Once they were there, he'd drag her to his room. Then he'd seduce all the information she held inside out of her treacherous body.

"I couldn't agree more."

"So I'm not to get new dresses?"

Rubina was not going to let the idea of new gowns go. He'd have to give into her desire at some point. But for the moment, what he wanted came first. She'd already played fast and loose with his emotions. She promised him she'd remain with him and give him an heir. He was afraid she'd run away before they could beget one. His greater fear would be she'd become enceinte and disappear again. Then he'd lose his wife and his unborn child.

Still, it was a risk he was willing to take.

Surely she wouldn't be as cruel as she appeared and deny him his one request. His gut churned at the idea. He was fast learning that anything was possible where his wife was concerned. Perhaps it was time to hire someone to watch out for her—or more apt to watch her period. He didn't trust her to not disappear again. He'd just fail to mention to her that she'd have a constant tail for as long as she remained in his house.

It was the only reassurance he could give himself.

"Not today. Perhaps I will gift you with some at a

later date." He smiled wickedly. "For now, you won't be in much need of clothing of any kind. I plan on keeping you in bed for the next several days."

Her hand flew to her chest. "Caro, you can be positively decadent."

Darling? She'd not called him such since she'd returned. Was she falling into old habits? He refused to acknowledge the endearment. His treacherous wife was not to be trusted, and Noah would not be lured into her web again. There was only one thing he wanted from her, and he'd enjoy every minute of it.

He'd not had a woman in years. The only one who aroused him was the deceitful bitch sitting across from him. So creating a child with her would be such torturous sweet pleasure.

The carriage stopped in front of their townhouse. Noah looked out the window. It was time to show her exactly what he expected from her. Rubina would be so well pleasured she'd be too limp from exhaustion to leave him for a while.

He kept his wicked grin in place, never once taking his eyes off of her. It was time for her to see exactly what he expected from her. He didn't hold back any of the desire flowing through him. The heat, the need, and the unwavering longing that had built up inside him while he believed she was dead.

"Darling," he enunciated the word, filling it with every sinful implication he felt. "I promise you, over the next several days, you will know exactly how wicked I can be."

CHAPTER EIGHT

ubina held her breath as she stared into Noah's heat-filled gaze. God help her, but she wanted everything they promised. She wouldn't fight him. He must know on some level that she wanted him just as much.

"I look forward to your,"—she tilted her lips into an enticing smile—"efforts…"

"Good, because we are going to start now."

"In the carriage?" She patted the seat next to her. "Oh, Noah, I didn't know you had it in you." She beckoned him with her finger. "Please, join me, and let's find out how wicked my husband has become."

Noah stared shocked for a second, then practically leaped at her. He pulled her into his arms and found her lips with his. The heat was instant and glorious as it spread through her. This is what she had been craving. The all consuming desire she could never resist—this is what she'd missed most when she'd lain awake in her lonely room. Heat was something she didn't feel a lot of in her prison.

Noah radiated enough to keep her warm for several years.

He trailed kisses down her neck as she entwined her fingers in his midnight hair. Every touch even more delicious than the last one—until he abruptly stopped.

Her eyelids flew open, and she met his lust filled gaze.

"As much as I'd like to follow you into carnal bliss, this is not the place to do it."

She raised an eyebrow. "Where's your sense of adventure?"

He laughed. "I will not be enticed into getting naked in the carriage with you, Ruby."

"Why not?" She pouted.

Just then, the door opened. A footman stood outside, holding it in place. "Do you need assistance, Your Grace?"

"No, Dobbins." Noah grinned. "We are ready to go inside." He leaned down and whispered in her ear," Is that reason enough?"

Her cheeks filled with heat. Noah had a point. This was not the place to fully reunite with her husband. "Yes, it is."

Noah stepped out of the carriage and turned to assist her out. He tucked her arm into his and led her into the townhouse. Simmons stood inside the foyer and nodded to them. He shut the door behind him. Rubina looked back at him after they had passed. She caught him with a huge grin on his face—like a cat enjoying the canary he'd caught. What did the normally stodgy butler have to smile about?

Noah didn't lead her to the sitting room. Instead, he turned down the hall to the staircase—leading to their bedrooms.

"Deciding to pick up where we left off in the carriage?"

Rubina couldn't wait to get him naked and at her mercy. The need to touch every inch of him welled up inside of her. It had been way too long since her husband made love to her. Her desire for him hadn't eased one bit.

"I already told you that I plan on keeping you in bed for days."

"Don't be ridiculous." She flashed him a smile. "That would be nearly impossible to do."

"And yet I intend to do just that." His gaze held so

much promise. "I wouldn't want to shirk on my duty to get you with child. The sooner my heir is born the quicker you can run off to your new love."

Rubina held her breath at his words. Slowly, she let it out. It would do her no good to stop breathing now. There was much she still needed to do. Shock had filled her—why, she didn't know. He only spoke the things she'd wanted him to believe. If only Paolo... No, Rubina wouldn't harp on what she couldn't control. Soon the man would pay for his treachery. Then she could tell Noah the truth and start to rebuild their relationship. For now—for his protection—she'd have to keep her secrets. When it was safe for him to know everything, only then would she unburden herself.

For the moment, she'd gladly take every ounce of what he offered her. It would have to be enough. It wasn't his fault she'd deliberately deceived him. This was her cross to bear.

"You're right, of course. The sooner I'm carrying your child the better."

She swallowed back the bile that filled her mouth at her lie. Part of her hoped she didn't conceive at all. What if she did and somehow Paolo got a hold of her again? Then he'd have her and Noah's heir.

He looked down at her with such derision it

made her heart skip a beat. The hate in his eyes hurt to see reflected back at her.

"Don't worry, dear. I will do everything in my power to make it happen as soon as possible. Once you're carrying my heir you won't have to stomach my attentions again."

Rubina bit her lip. Another reason for her to not want to conceive right away. She wanted to be with him in every way possible for the rest of her life. If she couldn't have his love, she at least wanted everything else. The idea of never feeling his arms wrapped around her again—it was almost too much to bear.

"Then, for your sake, I hope I conceive quickly. It must be difficult for you to have to make love to me knowing I no longer love you."

This pretense was killing her. The paleness of Noah's face at her words struck her heart with thousands of pinpricks. She didn't want to hurt him, yet she must. Soon, she'd let him know what was going on. After they located Paolo and made sure he'd never harm anyone she loved again. Then, and only then, would Noah know how much she still loved him. There would never be anyone else for her.

Noah dropped her hand and studied her a second. Then he started walking down the hall. Rubina followed closely behind him, unsure what he intended. He stopped just outside his bedroom door and turned to her. "It's a chore that will be worth it in the end."

He grabbed her hand and led her inside the room. Then he shut the door with a click and turned the lock.

"Don't want anyone disturbing us."

Rubina shook her head. "No, we have a reunion that must not be interrupted."

Noah frowned. "This is not a reunion. It's a necessity."

"However you wish to see it is fine with me." Rubina shrugged.

"Good. As long as we understand each other."

"I understand perfectly," Rubina said quietly.

Noah circled her as he studied every inch of her. Then he stopped behind her and started the long process of unlatching all the buttons of her dress. He pushed it down to the floor leaving her in her shift and corset. Soon, it too fell to the floor. The thin linen of her chemise was all that stood between her and complete nudity. Noah was still fully dressed.

"Aren't you going to remove your clothing too?"

"Are you in a hurry?" His gaze traveled over her.

Wetness pooled between her thighs. She wanted

to feel him sliding inside her, bringing her to ecstasy. She needed it more than words could say.

"Yes." She nodded.

"Too bad. I want to savor this moment."

"I thought you couldn't stand me."

Noah's actions were baffling her. What game was he playing with her? He didn't really want her, did he? He kept saying it was only to get an heir. This didn't require more than the actual act of intercourse.

"Some things need to be done, even when every part of you screams to run. I want you, Ruby, and I intend to have you..." He paused as he let his eyes roam over her again. "My way and in every way. You belong to me, and you will know it when I'm done with you."

Oh yes, she did belong to him. If he wanted to exert that control... She'd gladly let him. He loosened his cravat and pulled it free from his neck and tossed it on the bed. Next came his jacket, which he laid on a nearby chair. He opened a drawer and pulled out another cravat and tossed it on the bed next to the other one. He yanked the coverlet down enough to expose the sheet.

"What are you planning?"

"Not now…" He grinned wickedly. "But soon you will see."

He rolled the sleeves of his white shirt and stalked forward. He stopped in front of her. His fingers grazed her chemise so lightly she almost didn't feel his touch. Then he yanked her chemise off her body, leaving her completely naked in front of him.

"You're so damned beautiful."

He leaned down and licked one tight nipple. Rubina groaned with each sweep of his tongue over her sensitive flesh. Before she had time to react, he lifted her up and carried her over to the bed and lay her across the top. The cravats he'd tossed on the bed earlier were laying next to her head. Noah picked up one and wound it around her wrist and tied it to the bedpost—then did the other one.

"Have you learned a few tricks since we last saw each other?" She raised an eyebrow.

"For you, I learned many things."

Noah stood and stared at her for several seconds. It made her body heat up even more. If she reacted this way with just a gaze, she'd explode when he finally got around to touching her.

"Are you going to stare at me all day, or are you going to actually touch me anytime soon?"

She squirmed with need—resisting the urge to beg him.

"Perhaps it would help if you were blindfolded as well…"

He went over to his drawers again and pulled out another cravat. He tied it around her head, blinding her. This was a side of him she'd never seen before… and she liked it very much.

Since she couldn't see, the anticipation grew even more inside of her. So when she finally did feel him touch her, she groaned with the pleasure of it. The palm of his hand cupped her breast. He kneaded it, making her groan even louder.

"Do you like this?"

"Yes. Give me more."

Silence.

"No. You've been a very bad girl. You don't reward wickedness. You need to be punished first."

Oh, God. He was going to torture her with pleasure.

"I have been very, very bad. Perhaps you should spank me for my impudence."

"You'd like that, I think."

Noah pushed her legs open wide. Her knees were bent forward over her stomach. When his tongue touched the sensitive nub between her thighs, she nearly jumped from the intense pleasure. He kept licking over and over until she thought she couldn't bear it any more. Soon she'd explode around his sinful tongue. Then he stopped—leaving her unfulfilled.

"You were about to find your release. We can't have that yet."

Rubina cursed in Italian.

Noah laughed.

"You can't explode until I am buried deep inside of you, dear. It's the only way. Should we continue with your punishment?"

Sweat trickled down her forehead. He was killing her—it was glorious.

"Do your worst." She laughed. "I look forward to it."

"No, I don't think so." He joined her on the bed. The heat of his skin touched hers—the only indication she had that he was as naked as she was. "It's time we found bliss with each other."

Noah pushed her legs forward again. Slowly he pushed himself inside her tight channel. It stretched and burned, but it was the most wonderful thing she'd had happen to her in a long time. He stopped when he filled her completely.

"Wrap your legs around me," he demanded.

Rubina didn't need to be told twice. This was the only concession he'd given to her. He stroked in and out of her. Rubina moaned with each new thrust. Just when she thought she'd explode, he'd stop and suck one of her nipples into his warm mouth.

"Noah, please," she begged.

It seemed like forever. This constant battle of wills. He'd bring her close only to deny her the pleasure she sought. It was driving her mad.

"How much do you want me?"

"I want it all, Noah. Give it to me now."

"No, tell me you want only what I can give you."

"Caro, only you can bring me such pleasure. I need you. Make me explode in your arms."

Rubina would say anything he wanted to make him continue.

"All you had to do was ask."

Noah pumped inside of her in rapid strokes. The need built up inside of her again. She tensed, waiting for him to stop again. He didn't, and she saw stars burst apart behind her eyes. Rubina screamed as it hit her. Noah stopped as he found his own release and groaned in pleasure. It had never been so intense before…

"Grazie…"

Noah rolled off of her. He untied her hands and

removed her blindfold. Rubina was so weak she couldn't move a muscle. That had been the best... well...ever.

"You can return to your own room now."

He turned and walked into his dressing room, leaving her stunned.

What had just happened?

CHAPTER NINE

oah dipped his pen in the ink pot and wrote a few words into his account book. The words blurred in front of him. He tossed the pen down on his desk with frustration.

He couldn't stop thinking about Rubina.

Over the past month, they'd met in her bed chamber. He'd make love to her—leaving her weak and satisfied. As soon as they were done, he'd jump out of her bed as fast as he could. If he stayed, he would start begging her for things he knew she wouldn't give him.

He wanted her to stay—to love him like she used to.

This whole idea to have a child with her was slowly killing him. To have a small part of her wasn't nearly enough. If she didn't conceive soon, he'd be at her feet pleading with her. She already owned his heart. All he had left was his pride. Noah refused to give in completely to her. Surely she'd know if she were pregnant by now...

He'd ask her when he saw her again.

"For someone who prayed every day, for years, his wife would come back to him, you sure don't look like a happy man."

Noah looked up as Liam strolled into his study. For the first time in week he smiled.

"Where have you been?"

"At home." Liam's eyebrow rose. "You could have stopped by any time."

Noah sighed. "I've been busy."

Liam picked up a document and read it over. "Doesn't look too important. What's going on?"

"Rubina doesn't want to stay with me."

"I see." Liam sat down in front of Noah's desk. "Why?"

This was the hard part. The real reason he'd been avoiding visiting his best friend. How do you explain that the woman you married fell out of love with you? To make matters worse, she'd disappeared and let him believe she was dead for years. Only to return when she wanted to sever ties to be with someone else—a new man she claimed to love.

Even if she screamed his name each night as he made love to her. Noah had doubts she could possibly love the other man all that much. She crumbled at a mere touch from him. A woman in love with another man wouldn't be so ready to go to bed with someone else. Something wasn't adding up, but Noah had yet to figure out Rubina's game.

"She claims to love another."

"So why come back at all?"

Noah shrugged. "Hell if I know. She hasn't left the house the past month. I was going to hire someone to follow her, but she's stayed inside the entire time. It's baffling me."

"That doesn't sound like Rubina at all." Liam frowned. "Perhaps Gemma and Lily can get her to go out."

"Gemma and Lily?"

"Yes. Lily and Rand arrived a couple of days ago for a visit. Little William is a cute little tyke. Which reminds me..." Liam's lips twitched upward. "I'm going to be a father. Gemma just informed me she's pregnant."

Rubina might be pregnant... Part of him dreaded finding out. Then he'd have no reason to visit her bed again. It was the only thing she gave to him willingly. He both coveted and despaired the moment she'd inform him he'd be a father. If only he could look forward to it as Liam did.

"Congratulations." Noah smiled. "Now that's a reason to celebrate. I will get the brandy."

"No." Liam waved his hand. "I came by for a reason."

"Oh?"

"Gemma is having a dinner party. She's excited to have Lily around for a visit."

Noah didn't know if he wanted to drag Rubina over to Liam's for dinner. It might prove too much to have to pretend they were happy. Plus, he never did arrange to take her to a dressmaker. He'd have to rectify that as soon as possible. How was he to entice her to stay when he was being an abysmal husband?

"I see," he said. "When is this occasion to take place?"

"A few days' time." Liam smirked. "She'd have it tonight if she could make it happen. As it is, she'll be driving me mad for the next few days making all the arrangements."

"Who all is going to be in attendance?"

"My parents, you and Rubina, and of course Lily

and Rand," Liam explained. "It shouldn't be too bad. I know how little you like to socialize."

No. Dinner with Liam's family would be wonderful. They had always been a second family to him. He'd yet to meet Lily's husband, and he looked forward to it. She apparently was rather happy living in South Carolina and running the plantation. These visits were few and far between. Her son, William, would only be around a year old. Noah was a little surprised she'd decided to travel with him still being so young.

"Why did Lily decide to visit?"

"My parents haven't been able to visit. They meant to after Gemma and I returned, but the business has been busy, and Father hasn't found time to travel. Lily, being the headstrong woman we all know her to be, took matters into her own hands. She says her son needs to know both his grandfathers and made the trip over. Rand has his hands full with her."

Noah remembered how happy he had been when he brought Ruby home. He'd been so happy. No doubt Lily's husband was equally so. "I'm sure he doesn't mind."

"No, he loves her. The poor bastard." Liam

grinned. "I love her, but I kind of have to. She's my sister and all."

Noah wished he had a family as close as Liam. Some of the best memories he had were spending the holidays with him. The marriage of the Viscount and Viscountess of Torrington was wonderful to see. It was the kind he'd hoped to have some day—one he thought he'd found with Rubina.

How wrong he'd been.

So wrong it hurt to think about. There wasn't anything he could do to change it. The energy it took to hold all the tears inside was excruciating. It was a battle he'd been fighting his whole life. The only difference between his childhood and now was he'd made this choice. His parents hadn't decided to leave. They'd been taken away from him.

Rubina chose to leave.

"He's lucky to have your sister."

"Damn right he is. He knows it too," Liam said. "All in all, he's a good man. Lily chose well. It's a good thing she has him. Running that plantation is hard work. From everything they've told me, it's an uphill battle. There is a lot of tension still after the War Between the States ended. I wouldn't want to deal with it."

"Right." Noah tried to focus on what Liam was

saying, but it was getting hard to follow him. Something about Lily's home... "Is Gemma sending formal invitations?"

He had a lot on his mind. After Liam left he would arrange for the dressmaker to visit Rubina. She needed new gowns and one done fast. He didn't want her to feel out of place at the dinner party in one of her old dresses. She hadn't asked again, and he'd forgotten. It wasn't an excuse, but it's what happened.

"If I know my wife—and I do—she will. This is a heads up so you can prepare yourself. I know she's been wanting to come by and formally meet Rubina. Now that Lily is here, don't be surprised if she drops by one day."

Great, just what he needed to look forward to. Gemma had tact—Lilliana lacked it. She would blurt out what everyone else dared not. Noah had found it charming in the past. Now though, he dreaded it. He didn't want his life dissected. Was it too much to hope Lillian had mellowed since she married?

"How is your sister these days?" Noah asked. "I mean really. You said she's happy to be married and living with the heathens..."

"Yes?"

"Is she still the same spirited woman we always knew?"

"Did you miss the whole headstrong part of why she's here?"

"Right…" So he missed some important information while he'd been lost in thought. "I mean, is she as…blunt as she's always been?"

"I see. You want to know if she'd going to interrogate you or Rubina?"

Noah nodded. "I want to be prepared for anything. We all know how your sister can be."

"Well, then I'd prepare for her to storm the front lines, so to speak." Liam frowned. "She mentioned something about becoming reacquainted with Rubina. It didn't sound…good."

That was what Noah feared. Lily wouldn't let them get by with any deflection. When she asked a question she demanded an answer. Noah and Rubina had been getting along by not asking the hard questions. Perhaps it was time they were asked and answered. This impasse had been nice, but it was always doomed to crumble.

Noah sighed. "Duly noted." He scrubbed his hands over his face. What a mess.

"How are you doing really?"

"I'm not…" Noah didn't know how to answer

it. "No matter what I say I'm not over her. I want to be. But for me...time didn't erase my feeling. I don't know if I can convince her to stay."

"Do you want her to?"

Yes. He did. But not if she wasn't happy. The past month opened his eyes in a lot of ways. She went willingly to his bed, and he loved her in every way possible. He couldn't hold back while he held her in his arms. If showing her how he felt wasn't enough, nothing would be.

"It doesn't matter what I want."

"Don't be ridiculous." Liam crossed his arms across his chest. "If you want her to stay, fight for her. Don't give in just because she says she loves another."

"It's not that easy."

Liam didn't understand. You couldn't fight for someone who didn't want to be fought for. Rubina made her choice. Noah would let her go. If she wasn't already pregnant, he'd let her go sooner than he had planned. He wouldn't hold her to a promise he'd demanded in anger.

"Nothing ever worth fighting for is," Liam stated. "If you love her, then tell her. Show her that this is the place she belongs. She should never have left.

Make her want to be with you so much she lives and breathes it."

Was it possible? No, Noah wouldn't give in to false hope. It had already bit him in the arse hard. He shook his head. "Maybe you're right, but…"

Liam held up his hand. "No buts. Fight for her."

Noah let his mind roam to what it would be like if Rubina stayed. If she learned to love him again—to have children with her. Their lives so intertwined he couldn't see where she began and he ended. It was something he'd always wanted. He only dared to dream he could have it when he'd met her on his grand tour. When he first saw her… He knew she was the one for him. She'd been so beautiful in the moonlight. Their courtship had been fast, and he'd married her before he left. It wasn't until they got back to England that they'd started to fight. The realty of their life together hadn't been all sunshine and roses. Then, one day, she'd had enough and ran away.

He couldn't blame her. She'd been miserable.

"I don't know how to even begin to fight for her."

"You know Rubina better than anyone. Start there and woo her again. Show her that your love for her is enduring. You asked her for forever, and it's time she paid up."

Noah laughed. "You're right."

"You bet I am." Liam grinned. "I'm always right."

"Really?" Noah raised an eyebrow. "I'll have to ask Gemma about that when I see her again."

"Please don't." Liam shuddered. "I rather like sleeping with my wife each night. And with that, I really need to go home." Liam stood up. "Before I forget, I saw some strange man lingering across the street staring at your townhouse. Didn't like the looks of him. You might want to check him out."

"I will look into it." Noah frowned. Why would some ruffian be interested in his home? Were they thinking of robbing him? He would look into it later and order the house on full alert. "Thanks for coming by. I didn't realize how much I needed to talk to someone until you strolled through my door."

"Anytime." Liam waved as he left the room.

Noah sat back in his chair and steepled his fingers together. He had a lot of plans to make. His wife wouldn't know what hit her. Woo her? Oh, he intended to…

A siege of epic proportions was about to be enacted upon his wife—he couldn't wait to see her reaction.

For the first time in a month, Noah smiled. This was going to be fun.

CHAPTER TEN

*R*ubina lay on top of her bed. The room spun as soon as she'd lifted her head. Whatever caused the vertigo to hit her, she wished it would go away. Becoming incapacitated was not conducive to her plans. She needed to know what was going on with the search for Paolo. Damian had not come by, and she was nervous. It couldn't be a good sign. What if something nefarious had happened to him? She swallowed back her fear. Her brother knew how to take care of himself. She couldn't worry about him.

"Pardon me, Your Grace…"

Rubina turned her head, slowly. She winced with the effort. Damned nuisance this was.

"Yes, Abby?"

"There are two ladies here to see you. Should I tell them you're not available?"

Who could possibly be coming to see her? She had no friends—sad but true. No one came to visit her. It was usually busybodies or someone Noah knew. Although, this could be a way for Damian to reach her—he probably didn't want to get questioned further by her husband.

"No. I will come down. I can't lay about in bed all day."

She could—but she wouldn't. There was far too much at stake.

"Yes, Your Grace." Abby turned to go.

"Wait," Rubina called to her. "Please have some refreshments brought into the sitting room, and tell our guests I will be with them shortly."

She took a deep breath and rolled off the bed. First, she'd have to make herself presentable. Rubina sat at her vanity and gasped. She looked like death warmed over... She must be coming down with something. Perhaps she shouldn't visit with anyone —no it might be important. Whatever malady had overcome her, she'd take the risk. This social call could very well be a life or death situation.

Rubina pinched her cheeks in an effort to bring color to her porcelain skin. She sighed when it didn't seem to do much good. Hopefully her guests weren't so rude as to comment upon it. Hard to say—depending on who it was. If it was some busybody—God help them. Rubina didn't have the patience for them.

She quickly discarded her dressing robe and put on her burgundy gown. It was a good thing she'd gotten used to so little clothing choices over her years locked away or she'd have been highly irritated with Noah's refusal to visit the dressmaker. Suggesting it had been an excuse for why she'd been so distracted. What she'd actually been doing was scanning the streets for any unsavory individuals. Paolo's men could be lurking anywhere...

Time to go face the music...

Rubina descended the stairs and entered the sitting room. She held back her reaction to the visitors awaiting her.

"Oh, good. We were thinking you were intentionally avoiding us." Lilliana strolled across the room and pulled her into a hug. "I don't want you to think that we're cross with you. I'm glad to see you alive—even if you do look rather pale. Are you feeling all right?"

"Lily." Gemma gasped. "No need to be rude."

Lilliana shrugged. "It's the truth, so why not speak it?"

"I'm fine really," Rubina reassured them. The last thing she needed was for them to start asking questions. It would lead to places she didn't want to go. "I was resting."

"Why didn't you tell your maid you weren't feeling up to company?" Lilliana asked.

Gemma glared at Lilliana.

"Don't start, Gemma. It's a reasonable question."

Ruby laughed. She could tell the two women were the best of friends. She wished she could have had something similar, but it hadn't been her fate. Lilliana had always been outspoken, and she'd liked that about her. Too bad she didn't still live in England. It would be nice to call her a friend—if she got past her supposed betrayal of Noah.

"I thought it might be important. No one stops in to see me," Rubina interrupted them.

Gemma stopped to stare at her. Her mouth fell open as shock filled her green eyes. "Are you saying you've locked yourself away in this mausoleum and haven't gone out to socialize once since you returned?"

Rubina paused. How to answer that? With the truth? "I went out to visit my brother."

"That is just…wrong." Lilliana frowned. "What is going on inside of Noah's head?"

"Don't be hard on him. It's not been an easy month."

Rubina didn't want them to think badly of Noah. None of the tension between them was his fault. He was only reacting to what she wanted him to believe.

One of the maids pushed in a cart with tea and little cakes. The smell filled Rubina's nose, and she swallowed back bile that rose up her throat. She quickly covered her nose to block the offending odor… What the hell had they put in those foul cakes?

"Will there be anything else, Your Grace?"

She shook her head. The maid curtsied and left the room.

Rubina wanted to order the cakes removed, but Lilliana was already picking one up and popping it in her mouth. Gemma looked over at them warily.

"I think I will pass on the cake," she said. "Just tea for me."

"More for me," Lilliana piped in. "They are delicious." She turned to Rubina and asked, "You want one."

She waved it around in her vicinity just enough for he to get a good whiff of it—and send Rubina running in the opposite direction. She stopped by a nearby vase and lost what little contents remained in her stomach. The cake smelled so sickeningly sweet…

"Oh dear," Gemma stated. "How far along are you dear?"

Sweat dripped down her forehead. What was wrong with her?

"What?"

Gemma didn't make sense. Far along for what?

She tilted her head and studied Rubina.

"These things happen you know. There is no reason to be embarrassed. They say it only happens in the mornings, but they are wrong. It has hit me at all times of the day and sometimes the most innocent smells hit me hard." She turned toward Lilliana. "Why don't you carry the tray of cakes out of the room? They are a bit much for her weak stomach at the moment."

Yes. Yes, they were. How did she know? They were horrid little pieces of square monstrosities. She'd have to order cook to never make them again. Her stomach didn't react well to them at all.

"Oh, you poor thing. Why didn't you say something? I'd never have put them anywhere near you. When I was pregnant with William, I couldn't stand to be around eggs. I had to make cook promise not to make any for months." Lilliana picked up the tray and left the room.

"What is she talking about?" Rubina asked Gemma.

They were talking nonsense. What did eggs have to do with anything she wasn't pregnant...was she?

"Oh, you didn't know did you?" Gemma patted her on the arm. "Have you noticed any other signs?"

"Signs?"

This was all so confusing. They had to be wrong. She couldn't be pregnant. All right, she could—but it was unlikely. She never once conceived the whole first six months of her marriage. She'd begun to wonder if she was perhaps barren...

"Do you feel tender?" Gemma leaned in and whispered, "You know, on your bosom?"

Rubina jerked back in horror. This was not something she wanted to discuss, but now that she thought about it...

"I can't be..."

"Are you sure?" Gemma asked. "You and Noah haven't..."

"No, no, no. We are not going there." Rubina paced. "Yes, of course we have, but this just..." She stopped as a horrified thought entered her mind.

Noah would have no reason to make love to her again. He'd achieved his goal—and in record time.

Lilliana came back in the room. The tray was no longer in her hands. She stopped suddenly and stared at Rubina. "What's wrong?"

"She's a bit in shock. I don't think she realized she was you know…enceinte." Gemma gestured toward Rubina with her head.

"You can't tell him," Rubina said as panic seized her. "Promise me you won't say anything."

"It's not our place to tell Noah anything." Gemma frowned. "This is news that should come from you, but why don't you want him to know?"

Noah would distance himself even further from her if he knew she was carrying his child. This was what he wanted. He didn't really want her anymore. It was her fault—she'd made him hate her. After he made love to her, he practically ran away from her. He no longer held her afterward—it was an act of procreation. Even if it was hotter and more wild than it had ever been… She didn't want to give up the only reason she had to hold or touch her husband. He couldn't know yet. She'd tell him when she had no other choice.

"It's too soon…" What could she tell them that

123

would get them to agree? "I don't want to..." She waved her hands wildly. "You know..."

Gemma smiled. "I think I understand. Nothing is guaranteed, and you want to be sure before you tell him."

Rubina nodded. "Yes. That's it."

Noah would have expectations, and he'd get even worse with his dictations too. This baby—or the idea of it—was the only thing he clung to. She'd destroyed his love for her. It had been a difficult thing to do. No one—except maybe Liam—knew how he felt about family. He'd lost everyone he loved far too young. This child would be his only remaining link to having that back. Rubina was just the vessel to give it to him.

"Don't worry, your secret is safe with us," Lilliana reassured her. Gemma nodded in agreement.

"What secret?"

Rubina froze. How much had Noah overheard?

Gemma turned and smiled. "Noah, how good of you to come and see us while we're here. I thought you'd be too busy to bother."

Noah frowned. "I was just coming in to tell Ruby I have some things to take care of and I wouldn't be home for dinner. I had no idea you or Lilliana were here."

Lilliana pouted. "So you're going to run away and not even visit for a little while?"

These two were a tag team of distraction. Rubina had never been so grateful in her life. They had effectively changed the subject of any kind of secret. Maybe Noah hadn't heard what they'd been discussing. She could only hope...

He shook his head. "No. Now tell me what you three are hiding?"

No such luck.

Lilliana sighed. "If you must know, Rubina was telling us how you haven't allowed her to socialize at all. I mean look at her? Has she even seen sun in days? Do you keep her locked up in her room all the time?"

If she'd been talking about Paolo that would have hit the mark.

"Don't be ridiculous. Rubina can come and go as she pleases."

It was time for Rubina to steer him in a different direction. "In these rags?' She held up the skirt of her burgundy gown. "I wouldn't want the ton to think you mistreat me."

Gemma turned and studied her dress and continued where Rubina left off. "She does have a point. Why haven't you taken her to Madame Roussard's?"

"Ah, the secret isn't much of one now is it?" Noah smiled. "That is the other thing I came to tell you. I've arranged for Madame and her assistant to come by today and fit you for a brand new trousseau. Perhaps Lilliana and Gemma can help you choose some new gowns. Get whatever you want. Don't worry about the expense."

"Truly?" Rubina raised an eyebrow. "You're not saying that because we've guilted you into it?"

Noah grinned. "I would have done it sooner, but it slipped my mind."

Rubina didn't know what to make of his attitude —he was pleasant. Perhaps it was because his friends were visiting. Maybe he didn't want them to know how strained their relationship had become. If so, she'd willingly play the game for him. She didn't want to cause him any more undo heartache.

"Oh, this is going to be wonderful." Lilliana clapped her hands together. "I haven't gotten any new gowns in forever. Do you think she'd measure us all?"

Noah tilted his head and frowned. "Tell her to charge whatever the cost to my account—for the inconvenience. Tell her your own husbands can pay for your gowns. They can very well afford it."

"I'm going to pass for now. I'm going to need larger gowns soon. I might as well wait," Gemma said.

Noah smiled. "Liam told me your good news. Congratulations." He leaned down and kissed her cheek. "You will make a wonderful mother."

Rubina turned and stared at her. That is what she'd meant earlier. She'd not put two and two together. Her mind wasn't functioning as it normally did.

"Thank you." Gemma smiled. "One day you'll make a wonderful father too."

Noah's eyes grew distant at her words. Maybe he was remembering that she'd be the child's mother—or he believed he'd be raising their child on his own. Whatever the reason, Rubina didn't like it. She would never abandon her child. Her hand hovered above her stomach—Noah couldn't know yet. If she gave him any signs, she'd lose him entirely. She wasn't ready to let him go. Rubina let her hand fall back to her side.

"One day I may be lucky enough to have a child. For now, I will leave parenthood to you and Liam."

He smiled, but it didn't reach his eyes. "Now I must say goodbye. Enjoy your time with the dressmaker."

He turned on his heels and left the room.

He took her heart with him.

"All right, spill it. What is really going on between you two?" Gemma demanded.

Rubina turned to stare at her. "I'm afraid my husband no longer loves me, and I'm afraid it's very much my fault."

She burst into tears and ran from the room. Gemma and Lilliana could deal with Madame Roussard when she arrived. Rubina just couldn't handle any more company.

CHAPTER ELEVEN

The women were acting strange. Noah couldn't think about what that little scene had meant. He'd started the process; he needed to court his wife. He hoped his actions wouldn't prove foolish. Love shouldn't be so damned hard.

He scrubbed his hand over his face.

Thinking about the difficulties life had thrown him wouldn't get him anywhere. There were plans to be made. If he had any hope of winning Rubina's love again, he had to stop letting his thoughts drift down paths it shouldn't. Whatever had driven her away before—he'd do everything in his power to prevent it this time around. It was time to start considering it the gift it was. He had his wife back. For now, that was enough. Time was finally on his side. She wouldn't be running off until she gave him an heir.

Arranging for Madame Roussard to do a fitting in the comfort of their home was just the beginning. Maybe, with new dresses, he could coax her out of the townhouse and attend a few social functions. The first would be Gemma's dinner party. They appeared to be getting along, so Rubina would be less likely to object to attending. Then, after a while, they could start accepting offers to balls and soirees. Rubina used to be a social butterfly. Something was —different. Noah couldn't pinpoint it, but she seemed to be more content staying inside. The only time she'd willingly left was to go see her brother.

Another thing he must deal with. Damian hadn't been by. This secrecy between Rubina and her brother was irritating him. He had to know what they were hiding. So he had one very important errand on his list—someone who could help him get to the bottom of it all.

The carriage stopped outside a jewelry shop. Noah stepped out and walked inside. One of the first errands on his list—ladies loved jewelry right?

"Hello, Your Grace. May I help you."

Noah nodded at the jeweler. He knew him rather

well. It was the establishment he'd purchased all of Rubina's gifts before. The benefit of having a standing account with them gave him superior service. As long as he paid his bills, the jeweler's eyes lit up when he walked in. The last item he'd purchased was Pearla's engagement ring. He hadn't expected to return to purchase gifts for Rubina. It was odd, but good.

"I need to commission something special for my wife."

Noah could almost see the excitement twinkle from his eyes. A special commission would garner a hefty sum, but his wife was worth it. Nothing was too good for her.

"What did you have in mind?"

Noah explained what he wanted for Rubina. It was part of his big surprise. One that would take a lot of secrecy and planning—but he hoped in the end it would prove worth it. This was his whole life he was fighting for. He loved Rubina more than words could explain.

"Do you think it is possible?"

"Yes. It is very much possible. How soon would you require it?"

Noah thought about it. How to put a time limit on winning his wife back? This could tip the scales in his favor, but it was hard to tell. He could only hope.

"Can you have it ready in two weeks?"

"Certainly, Your Grace."

"Good." Noah smiled. "Now I'd like to look at your selection of necklaces."

"Did you have something in mind?"

"Rubies."

"I have just the thing." The man walked over to a safe, pulled out a black box, and then brought it back to Noah. "These were recently finished."

Inside, lying against black velvet, was a ruby pendant shaped like a teardrop. It was flanked by brilliant white diamonds trailing all the way to the clasp, a matching pair of ear bobs were nestled next to it.

"It's perfect." Noah gestured toward it. "Wrap it up. I would like to take it with me today."

"Certainly." The jeweler nodded.

Noah picked up the wrapped package and tucked it under his arm for safe keeping. "Let me know when my other item is ready."

"Yes, Your Grace."

Noah nodded and stepped out of the shop. One of his stops wasn't going to be as pleasant. It would take place in a seedier part of the town. Not a good idea to bring an expensive necklace with him. He went to his carriage and told his drive to take him to his club. He could put it in the lockbox there until he was ready to go home.

It didn't seem to take long before the carriage was stopping once again. Noah hopped out of the carriage and headed into Whites. He was immediately greeted by one of the club owners.

"A pleasure to see you, Your Grace. It's been a while."

"I've been busy. Can you put this in your lockbox until I'm ready to leave?"

"Yes, Your Grace."

Noah handed him the package and strolled into a private room. A waiter came by and took his drink order.

Liam strolled into the room. "I thought I saw you come in."

"Just a quick stop. I have a meeting in an hour."

"What for?"

"I'm going to hire an investigator. I need to know what happened to Rubina three years ago."

Liam frowned. "Don't you think it would be easier to ask her?"

Nothing about his wife's return had been easy. She didn't seem to want to talk about her time away

—other than to tell him she no longer loved him. Something was driving her. Noah needed to know what that was.

"Not at all."

The waiter set his drink in front of him. Noah picked it up and swallowed the contents.

"So you decided not to woo her?"

Noah shook his head. "I didn't say that. I've already started the plans to do that. Which reminds me—I need your help."

He explained to him what he had in mind. Liam would be instrumental in helping him pull a lot of it off.

Liam whistled. "When you decide to court a woman, you go big."

"If you're not going to do it right, why bother?"

"You make a valid point." Liam nodded. "Do you think it will work?"

It better. He was banking everything on it.

"I will do some little things to lead up to it. If she's willing to stay with me forever, then she will know in a couple of weeks." Noah could only hope it all worked as he foresaw it. "I have a plan, and I intend to have everything I want—including my wife."

"You think two weeks is enough time?"

Noah smiled. "She agreed to marry me in two days the first time I courted her. I think two weeks is plenty of time."

Rubina had shined brighter than the stars the first time he saw her. No other woman ever compared or ever would. Once she owned his heart, he knew he would never feel the same way about anyone else. He didn't give his heart to her lightly. Once Noah loved, it was forever. Now he needed her to see she still loved him too. He believed with everything he was that she still did.

"For your sake, I hope you're right. I know how miserable you were without her."

Liam only saw a little of how much he hurt after Rubina supposedly died. He'd lost himself for so long without her. His best friend picked up the pieces and put him back together—at least as much as Noah had allowed him to. He was never completely whole again. Rubina was his other half. Now he had her back, and he'd be damned before he lost her again. For a little bit, all he saw was his own injured pride. No more. It was time to do something instead of wallow in self pity.

"This will work. Tell me you can pull off your end."

"I can, but I don't know if I will be able to hide it from Gemma."

Noah smiled. "She can keep a secret. If I know your wife, she'll want to help. So tell her and enlist her planning abilities to my cause."

"Gemma does have a romantic heart—all right, I will tell her when I get home."

Noah laughed. "About that…"

Liam scrunched his eyebrows together. "Why don't I like the sound of that?"

"When I left, Lily and Gemma were about to help Ruby with a dress fitting. Don't be surprised if you get a bill from the seamstress."

Liam waved his hand. "That's fine. She'll probably need new dresses soon anyway and I don't mind the expense."

Noah understood. He'd buy Rubina the world if she'd take it. Whatever made her stay with him…

"I hate to cut this short, but I have a meeting to get to."

"Why don't I come along." Liam stood. "I don't have anything pressing to do."

Noah nodded. "I'm walking over. I will have to stop back here to pick up a package before I go home."

"Lead the way."

They exited the club and headed to a tavern down the street. The establishment they entered was a bit seedier than the one they'd left. It had a lot of commoners inside and bar maids that moonlighted as doxies.

"Can I help you guv'nor?" One of the maids approached them. She had stringy black hair and a very generous bosom—fully on display.

"I'm looking for Marcus Shepard."

"What you wanting him for?" Her lips pursed in displeasure. "He's not a fun fellow." She skimmed the back of her hand down his arm. "I can promise you pleasure you'll never forget."

Noah repressed a shudder. He only wanted one woman—his wife.

"Just tell me where he is."

"What about you?" She turned to Liam. "You like pleasure?" She wiggled her eyebrows suggestively.

Liam coughed and covered his mouth with his hand. After he got control over his laughter, he said, "I'm not looking for any amusements. Can you tell us where the gentleman is?"

The barmaid pouted. "Suit yourself. You don't know what you're missing. Marcus is over there at the corner table sitting by hisself. He don't much like company."

She walked way in a huff—clearly disappointed neither of them wanted the charms she offered.

"She's a character," Liam said.

"Not my type." Noah headed to the table Marcus was sitting at. "Hello, Mr. Shepard."

He glanced up—his gaze sharp and piercing as he studied Noah. "The Duke of Huntly, I presume?"

Noah nodded. "Yes."

"You brought company." He gestured toward Liam.

"This is Liam Marsden."

Marcus Shepard stared at Liam and smiled.

"The son of Viscount Torrington?"

Liam scowled. "You know my father?"

"We've—how do I put this—had business dealings in the past."

Liam held up his hand. "I don't want to know."

The man grinned. "Probably best you don't."

Noah didn't much care what Viscount Torrington hired him to do as long as he did his job well. "You come highly recommended. How good are you at tracking down information?"

"I'm the best." He tilted his head toward Liam. "Ask his father."

"I don't have to," Noah informed him. "He's the one that told me to seek you out."

It was Liam's turn to be shocked. He turned toward Noah and asked, "When did you see my father?"

Noah shrugged. "He stopped by a couple weeks ago. I told him about my concerns and he gave me a name to help me out. I'm just now using the information."

Viscount Torrington didn't ask for details. He'd taken one look at Noah and wrote down Marcus Shepard's name and handed it to him. Said when he wanted answers to seek him out. Now, it was time to finally find out what happened to his wife three years ago. It wasn't as simple as she made it all seem.

"What you need me to do?" Marcus leaned on the table. "I don't kill people, so we get that straight. I try to do things honorably—even if others in the company do some shady business from time to time —we all draw a line at killing people."

"I need you to investigate my wife's disappearance—three years ago. She returned suddenly, and it is all a bit—strange."

"I can do that." He frowned. "It will take some time. The trail is probably a bit cold at this point."

"You have two weeks," Noah explained. "I'm working on a timeline."

"That might be impossible—all I can do is try."

Noah nodded. "I also need someone trustworthy that can watch her when she leaves the house. I think she might be in danger." The man Liam had mentioned outside Noah's townhouse made him uneasy. He didn't know for sure if he meant them harm, but he had to be careful where his wife was concerned.

Marcus tilted his head and studied Noah. "I have a couple colleagues that will welcome the blunt. They are good at what they do. She won't even know they are there."

"Perfect." Noah stood. "One more thing. I don't want her to know any of this. So be careful when you send communications."

"I can be discreet." Marcus smiled. "It's what makes me so good at what I do."

"I look forward to your report." Noah tilted his head. "Until we meet again."

Liam got up and followed him out of the establishment.

"You really think Rubina is in danger?"

Noah didn't know why he felt it—but the niggling feeling wouldn't go away. It festered deep inside his gut whenever she was around. She was always nervous. Not once since she returned had she actually relaxed. His wife was so jumpy; even the smallest noise startled her. That spoke volumes to him.

"Yes. I don't know what's going on, but I will find out." He frowned. "I think this supposed lover of hers is a ruse. She's afraid of something, but I just don't know what it is."

They stopped off at Whites, and he grabbed his gift for Rubina.

"I hope it's not as serious as you think. When Gemma's cousin Alfie attacked me, the thought of losing my wife scared me. I don't know what I would do without her. I know you went through hell when you thought Rubina died."

They exited Whites and headed toward Noah's carriage.

"I know. I'm glad that all turned out well. You and Gemma are good together."

Liam smiled. "I have never been happier."

"Now I must return home to my wife." Noah stopped in front of his carriage. "I will see you in a couple of days at the dinner party."

Liam waved goodbye as Noah entered the carriage.

It had been a long and productive day. He couldn't wait to get home. The drive seemed longer than usual, but they were stopping outside his townhouse before he knew it. He hopped down and entered.

"Your Grace," Madame Roussard greeted him with a curtsy. She pulled on her gloves in preparation to leave. "I've gotten all the measurements I need for your wife's trousseau."

"Did it go well?"

"It did—I have to say the ladies with Her Grace were very helpful. It took a lot of coaxing to get her to do the fitting." Madame Roussard's lips formed a very thin line. "I was sad to see them leave. They had other appointments to get to."

Noah frowned. Rubina said she wanted dresses. Why would she refuse a fitting?

"But you were able to complete it?"

She nodded. "Indeed. I did say I got all the measurements. She was—rather weepy, but that doesn't matter for measuring."

"Can you have a gown ready in two days?"

She nodded. "I will send the first one over right away. I know she needs something for the dinner party. The rest will require some time to complete."

Noah didn't like knowing she didn't have the attire befitting her station. He should have done something sooner. His pride had made him into a terrible husband.

"Spare no expense. I want her to have some new gowns as soon as possible."

"Yes, Your Grace."

"The special dress…"

"Will be ready in time. You have my word."

Noah nodded. "Thank you."

Madame Roussard smiled. "No. Thank you, Your Grace. Your generosity will keep me in business for years."

She nodded and left the townhouse.

Noah stared down the hall. It was time to see what mood his wife was in and if she'd be receptive to the surprise he bought her. He'd never been so nervous in his life—even when he'd proposed to her. Back then Rubina had been a sure thing. Now she was anything but.

CHAPTER TWELVE

*R*ubina paced her bedchamber.

The seamstress and her assistant had left several hours ago. She hadn't been brave enough to leave her room and demanded a light meal sent to her. The idea of facing her husband—terrified her. How could she keep her pregnancy from him? All he wanted was to be a father. She destroyed any possibility of having a life with him. This was the one thing she could give him... But Rubina couldn't help the selfishness filling her heart. She wanted to feel his arms wrapped around her and the sweetness of him loving her each night.

If he knew she'd conceived it would be lost to her.

So, for a little while longer, she'd hold back the truth. Until she had no choice but to tell him she carried his child. Rubina rubbed her hand over her still flat stomach. It wouldn't take long before the evidence would be clear. She'd not be able to hide her growing belly. Their child nestled in her womb growing more each day—it was truly a miracle. Part of her was so happy her heart burst with excitement...

The other part of her feared the day she'd be forced to once again abandon her heart.

Paolo had to die. It was the only way she could have a chance with Noah and their child. She had to go see Damian. His absence was starting to make her nervous. What if Paolo had gotten to him? After Noah left her for the night, she'd sneak out to visit him. It was the only way she could ensure her husband wouldn't trail after her.

It was the first time she was grateful he left after he made love to her. There was a time when Noah couldn't leave her for even a moment—before she destroyed the love he had for her. Then, he'd hold her through the night, wake up, and make love to her all over again. These days he couldn't get away from her fast enough.

A light knock on her bedroom door startled her

out of her thoughts. Noah had come to make love to her again.

It was their nightly ritual. He'd pleasure her until she didn't think she could take any more, and then, he'd jump out of her bed as if scalded. Nothing hurt as much as seeing him run from her. It was her cross to bear. She'd made this choice, and she had to live with the consequences.

"Rubina?"

"Come in," she called out.

The door opened slowly. Noah peeked his head inside. "Are you all right?"

Rubina frowned. "Of course. Why wouldn't I be?"

Noah entered the room and shut the door with a soft click.

"The seamstress said you hadn't wanted to do the fitting."

Stupid Madame Roussard and her wagging tongue. Why did she have to go and tell him that she'd almost turned her away? At least Lily and Gemma had still been around to talk sense into her. Noah would have been suspicious if she hadn't ordered some new gowns. Now he was asking her questions she didn't want to answer.

"I was in a mood earlier. It has passed."

He studied her. "Why were you crying?"

Rubina struggled with the urge to look at herself in her mirror. How did he know? Were her eyes still red and puffy? "I don't know what you mean." Denial might still work if she played it well.

"Don't lie to me, Ruby."

Drat it. How was she going to distract him from this line of questioning? Maybe seduction was all she had left. She sashayed over to him and trailed her fingers down his chest. "Me, lie?" She batted her eyelashes at him coquettishly. "Why would I?"

"Ruby…"

She palmed his manhood. He hissed with pleasure under her ministrations.

"Yes, *caro?*"

"Don't think I'm letting this go." He wrapped his fingers around her wrist, halting her progress. She looked up into his eyes and saw the fire burning in within them. "I know what you're trying to do."

"I'm trying to entice you into my bed." She raised an eyebrow. "That should be rather obvious."

He lifted her hand and kissed her fingers. "We have time. We don't need to rush. Tell me what upset you."

Noah wasn't going to be so easily distracted. Why couldn't he let it go? She would have to try a different tactic to get him off this topic. She couldn't—wouldn't—tell him why she was so weepy.

"Don't we?" she asked, disgust filling her voice. "You seem to run away rather quickly once you finish with me each night."

He nodded. "I understand."

It was Rubina's turn to be confused. What did he understand? Rubina sure didn't. He was almost— nice. Her husband had been so indifferent toward her for weeks. Now he wanted to talk and show concern? Something changed; she just didn't know what it was.

She tilted her head and studied him. Compassion filled his warm brown eyes. She gulped back a lump in her throat. "Well then, please..." She flipped her hand backward. "Do explain this epiphany you've had."

"It's my fault."

Rubina frowned. What did he think was his fault? He wasn't to blame for the choices she'd made. He'd been wonderful considering...

"I must be daft because I have no clue what you're talking about."

He cupped her face in the palm of his hand. "I've been dreadful to you. I'm sorry."

Rubina stepped back out of his reach. Her heart

broke into a million pieces. She'd done this to him. He didn't know which way was up and what was down any more. This whole charade had made him doubt everything in his life. He hadn't hurt her—not intentionally any way. This was her doing. He'd never have put her through any of this misery if not for her lies.

"I don't blame you," she said softly. "The last several weeks have been trying on us both."

"No." He shook his head. "I won't let you absolve me of this guilt. I made you cry, and I have to make it up to you. I always did hate seeing you so sad."

"Noah, stop," Rubina demanded. "You are not the reason I was crying."

At least not directly…

He smiled. "So you admit it. You were crying earlier?"

Oh, drat—her husband was a clever man. How had she forgotten that? Rubina sighed. "Yes, I was crying, but it had nothing to do with you."

"So are you going to tell me what brought tears to your eyes?"

Rubina bit her lip. There was no getting out of this interrogation. How did she ever think she could? "No."

His head jerked back, startled. "No?"

"I'm not going to tell you. I don't care to discuss it."

Rubina had a stubborn streak, and she fully intended to lean on it. It was the only recourse left to her. Noah could take it or leave it—either way, she wasn't about to explain to him why her life was falling apart. She had to protect him and their unborn child. When the time was right, she'd tell him everything. Now was not that time.

He rocked back on his heels. "I see."

Did he? Rubina was afraid he saw far too much. "Good. Now do you want to do something more pleasant?"

"No."

It was her turn to jerk back. His words were like a slap to the face. "I don't understand."

"You don't need to." Noah sighed. "It's time we did things a little different. Somewhere along the way we lost sight of what we meant to each other."

Rubina nodded. She understood that much. The years apart—years they'd lost because of Paolo—had destroyed something between them. Her lies held the distance in place.

"I know."

"This whole time I've been trying not to love you —to need you—but I don't think it's possible. It's tearing me apart." Noah reached for her and pulled her into his arms. "It's making me need you—want you—so much more. It's not enough though."

"What do you want from me?"

Rubina was growing more and more confused with each word he uttered. This was a side of her husband she hadn't seen, well, since they married. They'd fought so much when they left Italy. England had bridged a gap between them—like a city divided upon itself. They were both stubborn and believed they were right. They had failed to compromise. Maybe this was the silver lining she'd been hoping for. If he was able to forgive her when he didn't have all the facts... There could be hope for them once they found themselves on the other side of the mess Paolo had made of their lives. Noah didn't know they had another battle to get through yet.

He pleaded with her. "I want a chance."

"A chance for what?"

"To win you back to have the life we originally planned." He started to unpin her hair. It fell down in blonde waves down her back. "To make you love me again."

Rubina gasped. "That's not possible."

Because she never stopped loving him—he couldn't make her feel something she'd never lost.

"It is, and I intend to make it happen."

"No…"

"Yes. This is a war I intend to win." He trailed kisses down her face and neck. "Trying not to love you isn't working for me—it only makes me love you more."

Her eyes watered, and tears trailed down her cheeks. She couldn't tell him she still loved him. Not yet. Still her heart soared to hear him say the words.

"Please, don't say these things."

They broke her. How could she keep her resolve when he tore down her walls with such sweet words? It would make it even more difficult to let him go if she couldn't find Paolo.

"I will say them every day until they sink in." Noah lifted her chin. Rubina refused to meet his gaze. "Look at me."

His voice was harsh. Rubina lifted her eyes to meet his. They were full of heat and a storm of need.

"Two weeks."

"What is in two weeks?" she asked.

"Give me two weeks. If I can't win your love back by then, I will let you go."

This didn't make any sense to her. What had changed? "What about your desire for an heir."

Noah let her go and took a step back. "We haven't

conceived by now. I think it's for the best. If you decide to stay, we can try again. For now, I think it is best we abstain from that part of our marriage. It was foolish of me to think to bring a child into a marriage on the brink of falling apart."

Rubina choked back a lump in her throat. He didn't want to make love to her anymore. This was all wrong... She should tell him, but what good would that do. Her husband now believed a child was the wrong thing to bring into their marriage. Stupid—so, so stupid—how could she have messed this all up so horribly?

"So what will you require of me then?" Rubina was almost afraid to ask. "If you no longer require a child from me, I'd like to know what this two weeks is for?"

Noah smiled. "Oh, we will share a bed. We will remain chaste for now."

"You need to explain what you want, Noah. This doesn't make sense to me."

"The simple answer is I'm going to court you."

Rubina frowned. "You don't share a bed with a woman you are courting."

"I realize that, but I have my reasons."

"I don't like this." Rubina paced the room. "What happens at the end?"

"If you still want to leave, I won't stand in your way."

"And if I want to stay?"

This was all rather—strange.

"Then I will do everything and anything to ensure you are the happiest woman for the rest of our life together." He stalked forward. Rubina took a step back. "And when I make love to you that night, it will be so good." He smiled wickedly, "…You'll beg me to give you more."

"What if I don't want to give you this time?"

"On this, I must insist. Two weeks isn't a long time. You were going to give me months before." He grabbed her again and pulled her back into his arms. "Say yes, Ruby."

How could she say no?

"You sure you don't want to make love?"

He laughed. "I think you're worth waiting for."

"So tonight we are just going to sleep together?"

He kissed her lightly. "I look forward to holding you all night. I've been denying myself the pleasure for way too long."

How had she gotten so lucky? Surely she had the best husband in the world. Rubina didn't deserve him, but she wasn't going to turn him down. Maybe this was for the best. At least she'd still have him with her each night. It would give her a little more time to deal with the Paolo situation. There was only one problem: she couldn't sneak away to meet Damian. She'd have to find another way to meet with her brother. It was time to deal with her nemesis once and for all. This was all driving her crazy.

As to Noah's request... She could at least give him the answer he sought.

"All right," she agreed. "I will give you your two weeks."

"I never doubted you'd say yes."

CHAPTER THIRTEEN

oah stared blankly down at the report Marcus had sent him. His wife had left the house in the early morning hour and went to visit her brother. She hadn't been inside long enough for a visit though. It appeared as if Damian had been out.

Noah couldn't help wondering where he was, but that wasn't his biggest concern.

Rubina had sneaked out of bed. Falling asleep with her nestled in his arms had been a little piece of heaven. Noah had been sound asleep when she decided to pay her brother a visit. It made him wonder how long she'd been planning to go to see Damian. Why was it necessary to go so early in the morning—well before regular visiting hours. Social calls happened in the late morning hours. The Albany didn't encourage female visitors before then. Noah was rather surprised she gained entrance at all.

This all had to do with whatever secret she kept from him. Marcus had better find some answers soon. He needed to know the truth. This pretending game his wife had going on was going to break them soon if he didn't. He scrubbed his hands over his face. This was becoming an obsession. Jealousy was an ugly emotion, and Noah had it flowing through him in waves. The problem was he didn't know exactly what he had to be jealous of. As the days went by, he firmly believed his wife didn't love another man.

At least not the way a lover did.

The strong bond she shared with her brother though—this secret had to do with him. Noah would bet his entire estate on it. Damian was at the center of it all. Whatever they were hiding was the reason Rubina closed herself off to him. It might not be entirely about her brother, but he did know the truth. It was that knowledge that drove his jealousy. She turned to her family—instead of him. For Noah, Rubina was his family. She was the one person he'd go through the fires of hell for.

They deserved to find happiness. Whatever tore them apart before had to be put behind them. Noah planned to see that happen one way or another. Rubina was his wife, and he intended on loving her for the rest of his days. No other woman would ever hold his heart. He didn't believe, for one second, she'd stopped loving him either. Whatever her reasons were for her lies had to be strong. She was too willing to walk into his arms and let him make love to her. A woman in love with another man would find a way to run in the opposite direction.

His wife practically begged him to love her—without saying the actual words.

That spoke loudly to him. What she wanted was perfectly in line with his own wishes. It was time he listened to the truth. This courtship idea was a way for her to see his words matched what he wanted for them. When Noah made a promise he kept it.

Now, as for her morning visit—she'd have to answer some questions. Her safety was his highest priority. He didn't want her sneaking out on a regular basis. There was always a chance the men he hired might miss her. Noah couldn't take a chance she'd slip away and some kind of harm come to her. He'd lost her once, and he refused to let something nefarious happen again. He folded the missive and put it in his desk drawer. It was time to have a conversation with Rubina.

Noah found her in the sitting room. Her face was rather pale. That seemed to be her usual hue lately. A momentary concern came over him as he observed her. What could be ailing her?

"Hello, dear," he said as he entered the room. "How was your morning?"

Rubina glanced up. "It was splendid. I paid Gemma a visit. I know we are going to be dining there this evening, but I wanted to get out for a little while."

The truth—but not the whole truth. Rubina had gone to see Gemma Marsden. She just made another stop first. He found it interesting she neglected to tell him about visiting Damian. It was one more reason he knew there was something big she hid from him. He would find out what it was soon enough. Noah wouldn't press her—yet. Part of him hoped she'd come to him with the information on her own.

"I trust you found her well?"

She smiled. "As well as a woman who is enceinte can be. She was a little green when I dropped in. The babe is making her ill in the morning hours."

"I'm surprised she felt well enough to visit." Noah

frowned. "If she was feeling out of sorts, she should have rested instead of entertaining."

"Gemma is perfectly capable of sitting down and having a conversation." Rubina glared at him, her voice filled with disapproval. "A woman doesn't become an invalid because she is carrying a child."

Noah rocked back on his heels. "I didn't mean to imply she was…"

Rubina interrupted him, "Furthermore, we are more resilient than you think we are. Women are capable of doing a great many things. We do not need to be coddled."

"I see."

And he did.

Noah saw things very clear. His wife was making a big deal over Gemma's pregnancy. It made him wonder if she wasn't telling him something… It would explain her pale complexion. Though he hadn't witnessed any other signs, it could be he was hoping for something that wasn't actually true. He wanted a child. More importantly he wanted one with his wife.

She nodded. "It's best you do."

"Oh, I assure you, I understand perfectly."

Rubina narrowed her eyes into tiny slits and

studied him. "What exactly do you think you understand?"

Bloody hell… He might have gone too far. It was time to distract her. "I noticed you left our bed rather early this morning."

She waved her hand dismissively. "I had trouble sleeping."

"You could have woken me up. I would have kept you company."

"No." She shook her head. "You slept so soundly. I didn't want to disturb your rest. I'm capable of seeing to myself."

Noah frowned. It sounded reasonable. Perhaps he was not seeing things as clearly as he'd thought. She seemed fine. Even the color was returning to her cheeks. Sometimes he just saw what he wanted to see. In this case maybe he was only hoping his wife carried his child… She seemed as resilient as she claimed.

"Did you go anywhere else this morning?"

"No."

She lied. Why would she hide her visit to her brother? It didn't make sense.

"Damian hasn't been by. I thought he said he would come for a visit."

Her head jerked up. Fear filled her eyes—she

quickly hid it. Not before he saw the flash of it fill them though. Rubina was worried. When he responded to Marcus's missive he'd add another assignment. Damian needed to be found.

"I'm sure he found something to keep him busy."

She hid it well, but Noah knew her. Her lower lip quivered a tiny bit before she answered him. Rubina was worried something had happened to her brother. What though—Noah could only guess. Maybe it was time to push her to give him the answers.

No. She would close up even more. It had to be her idea.

"You're right. Damian always did follow his own path. No doubt he's found something amusing to keep him busy over the past several weeks." He bowed his head toward her. "If you'll excuse me, I'm going to change for dinner."

"Yes. I should retire to my chambers as well." She stood up next to him. "My new gown was delivered this morning. It's beautiful—the color of rubies. Madame Roussard is a genius with the needle."

"I'm glad you liked it." Noah smiled. She would like his other gift to. He intended to fasten it around her neck himself after she was dressed.

"It's lovely." She smiled. "Perhaps the prettiest gown I've ever owned."

"Come, I'll escort you up to your room." Noah held out his arm to her.

Rubina smiled. "I'd like that."

They strolled up the stairs. He stopped just outside her room. She glanced up at him through a hooded gaze. She seemed to be waiting for something from him.

"I'll meet you downstairs when it's time to depart."

Disappointment filled her eyes as he took a step back.

"Yes." She toyed with her hands, anxiety filled her voice. "I…"

Noah pulled her into his arms. A small gasp escaped her lovely mouth. He took the opportunity to press his lips against hers. Her fingers quickly wound around his neck, allowing him to pull her further into his embrace. The kiss was filled with so much passion it burned inside of him. If he pushed it, they'd be making love in her room in mere seconds. He wanted to strip her and kiss every inch of her.

But he had to be strong. This was a courtship. It didn't matter if they were married. He had to show her respect. Make her realize she could trust him and that he would always keep his word. They would have nothing if she couldn't learn to believe he'd always protect her.

So he took a step back. It was the hardest thing he'd ever done.

"Why did you stop?"

Her breathing was ragged and desire shone brightly in her eyes.

Noah smiled. "I can't very well ravish the woman I am courting. It wouldn't be proper."

Rubina pouted. She ran her fingers down his chest. "I wouldn't mind. I like it when you're not entirely proper."

Noah laughed. He leaned down and placed a quick kiss on her forehead. "Not tonight, dear. We made a deal, and I am sticking to it. Now, be good and I'll bring you a present in a little while."

Her lips tilted into a coy smile. "Does it involve you giving me something I really want?"

"Please," he begged. "I'm only a man—flesh and bone. I can only take so much temptation before I give in."

"One would certainly hope so." She cupped his cheek in the palm of her hand. "You know you want to kiss me again. Just one little kiss...

What could it hurt?" She blinked her eyelashes at him as she flirted. "Kiss me like you mean it, Noah."

How could he say no?

So he swooped down and kissed her as if his life depended on it. The truth was it very well might. He could stop at any time. She was his drug—one he willingly succumbed to. How did he think he could survive two whole weeks without making love to her? Somewhere along the way he'd lost his bloody mind.

He tore himself away from her. Her lips were plump from his kisses... It made her even more beautiful to him. Noah shook his head and took several steps back. If he didn't, he'd pull her back into his arms, and then there would be no turning back.

"Love me, Noah."

He jerked his head up and met her gaze. It was filled with such decadent promises. Ones he knew she could and would fulfill if he took her up on them. He couldn't though. This had to go the way he planned. It did not include him giving in a little more than a day.

"Always..."

"Then join me. Show me how much."

"No," he croaked, his voice raw with emotion. "Don't ask me again."

Noah spun on his heels and headed toward his room. One more second and he'd have been stripping every piece of clothing off of Rubina. Then they'd never make it to Liam and Gemma's dinner party. The tether he had on his control was slipping each moment he spent in her company. Soon he'd be on his knees begging her to love him. When that day came he hoped she took pity on him.

If Rubina refused to admit she loved him… Noah would be lost for good.

CHAPTER FOURTEEN

*R*ubina sat in front of her vanity staring blankly at her reflection. She would have to move soon. Noah was probably already waiting for her… The dinner party should be something she looked forward to. It was meant to be a light evening amongst family and friends. Instead, she had other worries.

Noah was being rather lovely. Every moment she loved even more than the one before, but she still couldn't bring herself to tell him everything. A decision had to be made. Damian wasn't in his rooms. She'd checked when she attempted to visit him.

Where could he be?

"Trust me, you couldn't be more beautiful if you

tried." Noah leaned down and kissed the top of her head. "What's troubling you?"

She had been so lost in her own thoughts that she hadn't heard him approach. Rubina bit her bottom lip. The truth on the tip of her tongue—she swallowed it back. This wasn't the time. Without all of the facts, she couldn't spill her innermost fears.

"I'm not sure I'm up to company tonight."

Truth… The idea of spending time laughing with friends was the last thing she needed. Damian's whereabouts was her biggest concern. She should have gone looking for him sooner. If she had…

"Maybe my gift will help lighten your spirits."

Rubina turned. He held a black velvet box in his hands. "What is it?"

She could guess. It must be jewelry of some sort.

"Open it up and see." He handed her the box.

Her husband shouldn't be giving her gifts. She didn't deserve them… With hesitation she opened the lid. Inside was a brilliant diamond and ruby necklace—matching her gown to perfection. How had he known?

"It's beautiful…" Her hand flew to her throat. "How?"

Noah's smile lit up his whole face. Rubina sucked in a breath. He was so handsome and he looked…

happy. She hadn't seen a true smile on his face since she returned. Her heart lightened a little at the joy in his eyes. It might not solve all of her problems, but for the moment it was enough. She could give him this night. Tomorrow was soon enough to worry about her brother. Damian could be deep undercover. He'd surface when he had information. These were the things she told herself to get through the hard moments.

"You have your secrets," he replied. "Let me have my own."

Rubina's lips tilted into coy grin. "All right. For now, *caro*."

She touched the necklace lightly. It was so beautiful.

"Here, let me put it on you."

Noah lifted it off the crushed black velvet and placed it around her neck. The ruby teardrop nestled above her chest. Her husband didn't know how appropriate his gift was. The teardrop was a good representation of all the pain she suffered without him. She'd have to look at it for the present it was. There would be no more tears filled with pain—instead, they'd be full of joy. The ruby would be her reminder of all the good things to come.

"Thank you," Rubina whispered.

Noah kissed her cheek. "I would do anything for you, Ruby. Remember that when you look at this." He let his fingers roam across the diamonds and rested briefly on the ruby. "Our future holds so much promise. I look forward to spending it with you."

Rubina fought back the tears that threatened to spill from her eyes. She stood and turned toward Noah. She wrapped her arms around his waist, rested her head against his broad chest, and held on tight.

"Are you all right, Ruby?"

"I'm fine. I just wanted to hold you for a moment."

She started to step back, but he wrapped his arms around her. He brushed her back with the palm of his hand. "I could get used to this.

She lifted her head and stared into his warm brown eyes. "What?"

"These impromptu moments of affection." He smiled. "Keep this up and we won't need a whole two weeks."

Rubina wished she could end the charade now. She didn't need two weeks to know what she wanted. She'd always wanted Noah. Stupid Paolo... This would end—and soon.

"We should go, or we'll be late."

Rubina stepped out of his arms and headed down the stairs. She didn't turn to see if her husband followed. Noah wouldn't be far behind. He'd been open and honest with her since he made his deal. He wanted her, and he'd follow her wherever she led. Soon she'd be doing the same.

"Is the carriage ready?" Noah asked the butler.

"Yes, Your Grace."

Noah nodded and helped Rubina into her pelisse. They exited the townhouse and stepped into the carriage. Liam and Gemma didn't live to far away. Soon the carriage stopped to drop them off. Rubina took a deep breath. She'd need all the help she could get to make it through the evening. Tomorrow, she'd figure out what happened to her brother. Tonight was all for Noah.

"What's on your mind?" Noah asked as they approached the entrance.

"I was wishing for a wonderful evening. It's been a while since I've had a pleasant one."

Understatement... Paolo had made her life miserable. She loved Noah, but since her return, their relationship had been quite strained. Not his fault—but it was still the truth.

"Everyone should be here. I know Lily and

Gemma will do everything they can to make it enjoyable."

The door swung open. "What are you two doing standing on the door step. Come in already."

Viscount Torrington held the door open. Noah's mouth hung open in surprise.

"Why are you answering the door?"

His eyebrow rose mockingly. "Are you giving me lip, boy?"

"I would never." Noah smiled. "Where's Pemberly?"

"There's been some disaster in the kitchen… Gemma is having fits. He's following Liam around, intervening where he can." Torrington laughed. "My son has turned into an idiot since he found out she's carrying his child. It's rather amusing to watch."

"Liam is in the kitchen?"

"He is wherever Gemma is." Viscount Torrington motioned for them to come inside. "Hello, Rubina. It's lovely to see you again."

They stepped inside as he shut the door behind them.

Rubina smiled. "It's been too long."

"Oh, there you are." Lady Torrington strolled into the foyer. "I thought you were going to get Liam."

"Soon enough, dear." He kissed her cheek.

"Someone had to answer the door."

Rubina watched their interaction. That is what she wanted with Noah. The love they held for each other filled the room. No one would doubt the affection they had for each other. They were a lovely contrast. Pia, Lady Torrington, stood next to her husband with such grace. Her blonde hair so fair it was almost white and her husband's as dark as sin. Thor, Viscount Torrington, only had eyes for her. Someday, when people looked at her and Noah, they would see something similar.

"I apologize." Lady Torrington approached them. "Liam can't seem to let Gemma handle anything on her own these days. Please, join us in the sitting room. Lily and Rand are already inside."

Noah nodded. "I can go and find Liam if it will help."

Torrington patted him on the back. "Not at all. I will go and get him."

"Come with me." Pia gestured to them. "Lily has been waiting for you to arrive."

The viscount went in the opposite direction.

"Finally," Lily exclaimed. "I thought you'd never get here."

She grabbed Rubina's hand and led her over to the settee. "So have you told him yet?"

Her gaze shot up to her husband. He was in a deep conversation with a dark haired gentleman. "Is that your husband?"

Rubina had never met Lily's husband, Rand.

She glanced over her shoulder and smiled. "Handsome devil, isn't he?"

"I..."

How did she answer that? He was indeed handsome, but to her, Noah would always be the best looking man in the room.

"Oh, I know that look. You love your husband, but surely you can appreciate a fine piece of male flesh still." She waved her hand. "Rand was such a gentleman when we met. Wouldn't make love to me until we said our vows. It was so frustrating." She smiled, her eyes glazing over for a few seconds. "It was worth it in the end. His patience is what made me love him even more."

Rubina bit her lip. She understood, more than she was willing to admit. She was going through something similar with Noah. Why he felt the need to have this moratorium on making love she didn't know, but she respected him even more for it.

"Rand is rather handsome," Rubina admitted. "But you're right. Noah is the only one for me."

"So, have you told him?"

"What?" She tilted her head. What was Lily asking?

"About the baby?"

"Oh…" She shook her head. "No. I told you it's too soon."

"When we left, you were so sad. You said that you were losing him." Lily glanced at Noah. "From what I can see that man only has eyes for you. Are you going to tell me what's going on?"

Could she trust Lily?

"I can't speak of it." It wasn't a good place to divulge secrets. "There are too many ears here."

"I understand." She nodded. "I will pay you a call tomorrow. We can speak them. I will bring Gemma."

"Did I hear my name?" Gemma sat down on a chair near the settee. "Liam is driving me mad. Someone put him out of his misery."

Lily laughed. "Men are such babies. He doesn't know what to do with himself. Have pity on him. He can't help it."

Ruby didn't have experience with this…bonding. She'd only begun to get to know Lily before Paolo abducted her. Gemma was a mere acquaintance.

"What is he doing?" Rubina asked.

She should know what to expect once she told Noah she carried his child.

"What isn't he doing?" Gemma blew out an exasperated breath. "He hovers, he orders, he tells me he loves me every day."

"That…doesn't sound too bad."

"Just wait. When Noah realizes you are carrying his child you will understand. It's almost as if Liam thinks if I breathe too hard I'll break. I'm pregnant not an invalid."

Lily patted Gemma's hand. "It will get better. Wait and see what happens after the baby is born. He'll have something else to focus his attention on."

"One can only hope." Gemma rolled her eyes. "In the meantime, if Liam doesn't stop, he might find himself tied to the bed for the rest of my pregnancy."

"Gemma, love." Liam leaned down and kissed her lips. "If you wanted to get creative, all you had to do was ask. I'm open to suggestions."

Gemma glared at her husband. "Be careful where you tread. I'm still mad at you."

"Don't stay mad long." He grinned wickedly. "What fun would that be?"

"Hmmph…" But no one was fooled by it. She loved her husband too much.

Rand and Noah joined them. Rubina's gaze met her husband's. She wanted this. All of it and everything that came with it. Noah smiled at her. It was almost as if he'd read her mind. He was saying so much with that look. Say yes, Rubina. If she gave in and admitted it all she could have him and friends too.

"Dinner is served," Pemberly announced.

Noah helped Rubina up. Everyone headed toward the dining room. He leaned down behind her and whispered in her ear, "Has the evening met your expectations so far?"

His breath was warm against her ear. She shivered as tingles of energy flowed over her body. Yes. Yes, it had... But Rubina was selfish. She wanted so much more than this. She wanted to turn into his arms and beg him to take her home. Noah was hers, and she wanted to claim him once and for all. If only...

"I can think of only one thing that would make this better."

"What?"

"Another time, *caro*." She smiled. "I will tell you in explicit detail what I want to do at the end of an evening such as this." Rubina turned in his arms and spread her hands across his chest. "But you don't want to do anything close to what I have in mind for several days." She let her hands slide under his dinner jacket. Just a little tug and she could roam her hands against his warm skin—she held back the urge. She stared up at him and licked her lips.

His breathing was ragged. "You're correct."

"You know where to find me when you change your mind." She stepped out of his arms. "Dinner's waiting."

She left him standing in the middle of the sitting room. Rubina didn't look back as she headed toward the exit. If she did, she'd be dragging him out of Liam and Gemma's townhouse, demanding he take her home. They both wanted each other. Why they fought it... Rubina still didn't fully understand her husband's motives.

"Rubina," he called after her.

She turned around and sucked in a deep breath. He looked so...decadent.

"Yes?"

He strolled to her side and looped her arm through his. "This isn't over." Her husband leaned down and whispered in her ear. "I will have you again, and when I do..."

She looked up into his eyes again. A mistake—heat flooded through her.

"I will know all your secrets," he promised. "What's more, you will willingly give them all to me."

Rubina was afraid he was right.

CHAPTER FIFTEEN

*S*unlight streamed through the window of his study outlining the parchment on his desk. He cupped his mouth with his hand as worry filled him. Noah picked up the note that Marcus had sent him and read it over again.

Your Grace,

We need to meet in person. I know what happened to your wife. I will be in the tavern awaiting your arrival. Come with all due haste. It could be a life or death situation. There is some serious criminal activity afoot.

Don't waste time,

Marcus

Noah folded the missive and put it in his pocket. He walked out of his study and ran into Liam, almost knocking him to the ground.

"What's the rush?" Liam grabbed onto the wall to steady himself.

"I need to go meet Marcus. He has news."

Liam nodded. "I will go with you. I'm admit to being rather curious. By the way—I did ask my father about him. He was closed mouth. Makes me wonder now what the man did for him."

"I don't know if I want to know." Noah shook his head. "But I trust your father's instincts about people. He hasn't survived this long dealing with fools."

"You're right about that." Liam grinned. "I'm sure his years as a pirate served him well."

"Let's go. Marcus's note indicated it was important I meet him. I don't want to waste any time chatting here. Not with my wife's life at stake."

Liam nodded and followed him out the door. "My carriage is out front. We can take it and save some time."

"Good idea."

Noah gave the driver instructions where to take them. They got inside for the quick trip to the tavern they previously met Marcus at.

"Did he tell you anything in the note?"

Noah shook his head. "Not much."

He pulled it out of his pocket and handed it to Liam, who whistled.

"This doesn't sound good at all."

Noah was worried. A sick feeling filled his gut after reading Marcus's words. What could Rubina and Damian be involved in? It had to be bad for the man he hired to be concerned. He didn't seem to get stressed out about much. This had to be incredibly serious.

Noah clenched his hands into tight fists. No one was taking Rubina away from him ever again—he would not live in that hell for the rest of his days. He was finally starting to feel alive again.

Rubina was his.

"Whatever it is, I will face it. If it means keeping my wife safe, I will kill the devil himself." Noah's lips were a firm tight line. "Nothing and no one will ever take her away from me again.

Liam nodded. "I will help you in any way I can."

"I know." Noah tilted his head. "I appreciate it."

The carriage came to a stop. They got out and headed toward the tavern. They saw the same buxom waitress that flirted with them the first time.

"Did you two have a change of heart?" she asked. "I'd be willing to take you both on at the same time.

Just say the word." Her lower lip lifted into a sexy pout.

"No, we're here for Marcus again." Noah dismissed her.

"He isn't here."

Noah's head whipped around. "What? Where did he go?"

She shrugged. "He hasn't been by in days."

"That seems…odd." Liam stared at Noah. "What do you want to do?"

Panic settled into his gut. Why would he send him the missive and not show up to their meeting? Something was wrong…

"Let's go back to my place. We can figure out what to do from there."

They turned to leave as Marcus stumbled into the door. He held his side as he limped over to them. He gasped for breath and almost fell at their feet. Liam reached out and steadied him.

"What happened to you?"

"Duca d'Sordillo." He groaned. "He means business."

"Who is that?" Liam asked. "It sounds familiar."

Noah paled. Damian had mentioned his name on one of his visits—before Rubina returned home. He had been courting her before she met Noah. The man had offered for her, but Ruby turned him down. She never said why. Damian mentioned her father wouldn't have approved either way. He had some nasty business dealings, and there were a lot of rumors surrounding him. If he was involved it couldn't be good, and it might explain why Rubina was so afraid. It had never occurred to him that he might be. Why would it? Noah had won her hand and married her. How obsessed was the duca with his wife?

"Is he in London?"

Marcus nodded. "He is here to take Rubina back to Italy."

"I don't understand…" Noah looked around the room. "Perhaps this isn't the best place to talk. You need medical attention. We can go back to my town-house, and I will send for a doctor."

"Brilliant idea, Your Grace." He shook his head. "Only one problem with that. Rubina is at your house and every person the Duca d'Sordillo wants to get his hands on will be in one place." He coughed hard and a drop of blood fell on his lips. "No, take me to a room upstairs. I keep one here. I will tell you everything there. Don't worry about your wife. My men are still keeping an eye on her. No one will get to her inside your home."

Noah and Liam helped him up to this room and laid him on his bed.

"Your wife—as you know—did not go down with the ship she supposedly died on."

Noah frowned. "Tell me something I don't know. What is going on."

"D'Sordillo has been obsessed with her for years. He meant to marry her himself."

"Again, tell me something I do not already know. This is all old news."

The man grimaced and clutched his side again. "If you knew that much, why didn't you tell me. Would have saved me a lot of time and maybe prevented the knife to my gut."

Noah waved his hands in the air with frustration. "I didn't know the man was crazy or obsessed. I figured he'd moved on."

Marcus kept shaking his head back and forth, remaining silent for several seconds. "I thought you were a lot smarter—forgive me for assuming too much."

"I don't have time for this. Tell me what you found out," Noah demanded.

"Give the man some space," Liam urged. "He is bleeding a bit there."

Noah opened and closed his mouth. "You're

right. I apologize, but all of this is making me insane with worry."

"Yeah and to think it's only going to get worse now that Rubina is carrying your child." Liam frowned. "Trust me, I know. Gemma is about to pummel me for hovering over her."

"What?" Noah turned, shock filling him. "Ruby isn't pregnant."

"Oh, you didn't know?" Liam's mouth fell open in surprise. "I would have thought... Gemma knew... I just assumed. I'm sorry. That shouldn't be news you heard from me."

Why wouldn't Rubina tell him?

"Sounds like you have even more reason to keep your wife safe." Marcus sat up. "D'Sordillo is going to try and kill you—and he will take her again."

"Again?" Noah asked. "Is he the reason she's been gone for so long?"

"Yes," he replied. "She escaped by chance. Damian had men watching him for different reasons. When one of his men discovered that Rubina was being held captive, he helped her get away. That was when her brother found out she was alive."

"How long ago?" Noah asked, swallowing a lump forming in his throat.

His wife was pregnant, and danger loomed over her head.

"A couple of months…" Marcus paused. "I'd estimate a few weeks before you were about to remarry she managed to find Damian. They sailed to Florence first and then headed straight here. From that point I'm sure you know the rest."

"I'm still confused." Noah paced the room. "Why would she want to divorce me."

The man laughed and then grimaced in pain. "I suspect it was because she loves you."

Noah turned and shouted, "You don't divorce someone you are in love with."

"You do if you're trying to protect them," Liam said softly. "Duca d'Sordillo means to kill Noah as long as he's married to Rubina, doesn't he?"

Marcus nodded. "He might not have if Rubina hadn't escaped, but now that she's home with her husband—yes, that is indeed his plan."

Noah rubbed his hand over his mouth and let their words sink in. It made sense. He wanted to wring her neck. How could she not have told him all of this? She knew how much he loved her. They could have dealt with this together. Instead, she kept it all to herself and left him blind to the situation. At least he had Marcus to thank for filling him into what was really going on with his wife. Otherwise, he'd still be left in the dark.

He started to laugh manically.

"Are you all right?" Liam asked.

"She does still love me." He grinned. "She's got a strange way of showing it, but she never stopped. This is all insane—she might even be a little mad. But you know what? It doesn't matter because she's all mine."

"What are you going to do?"

"I'm going to go home and have a little chat with my well-meaning wife and explain to her why she shouldn't lie to her husband." Noah started to leave.

"Wait, Your Grace," Marcus called out. "There is something else you need to know."

Noah stopped in his tracks and turned. "What?"

"d'Sordillo has Damian." Marcus grimaced. "It's why I was stabbed. I got too close. The good news is I know where they stashed him."

"What's the bad news?"

"It's guarded so well it might as well be a fortress."

Noah cursed. This had gone from bad to worse. How was he going to get Damian out of this mess? They should not have kept him in the dark for so long. What was d'Sordillo involved in that made

Damian think he needed to keep an eye on him anyway?

"What is inside that they need so many guards?" Noah asked. "Surely it isn't just to watch over one man."

"I'm not entirely sure what they are guarding." Marcus swung his legs over the side of the bed and sat up. "I suspect it's more for protection than anything. Paolo Fonte, Duca d'Sordillo is high up in the Italian mafia."

"Bloody hell." Noah paced the room again. "This is damned mess."

"Where do we even begin to rescue Damian?" Liam asked.

"I'm not sure you can." Marcus shook his head. "He might be lost to you."

"I refuse to believe that," Noah said.

Rubina would be devastated if anything happened to her brother. Noah knew that Damian was high up in the Italian government—but, at the heart of it, he was protecting his sister. It might have started as an investigation into his criminal activities —that would have all changed when his sister found him. It was now up to Noah to finish what he started.

"One more thing, Your Grace," Marcus said. "The orchard you purchased in Sicily."

"What about it?"

"D'Sordillo wants it. I don't know how, but it's key to whatever plans he has."

"He bloody well can't have it or my wife." Noah growled.

No one took what was his. It was time Paolo Fonte realized that.

"Let's go. I need to check on Rubina."

Liam nodded. "Right behind you."

Noah stopped, turned toward Marcus, and said, "Thank you for finding out everything I needed to know. I will make sure a doctor comes to help you."

"Don't worry about me." Marcus grinned. "I have my own saw bones that sees to my needs. One of my men has already gone to get him. Go look after your duchess."

Noah nodded and headed out the door.

It was time to raise some hell—starting with his wife.

CHAPTER SIXTEEN

"*P*ardon me, Your Grace." Simmons entered the sitting room. "This arrived for you."

"What is it?" Rubina asked.

"I'm not at liberty to say." Simmons shrugged. "I don't read my employer's missives."

Rubina rolled her eyes. "All you had to say was someone sent me a note. It's probably from Lily. She was supposed to pay a call today. Give it to me."

She broke the wax seal and read over the contents.

DUCHESSA,

Paolo has your brother. Meet me at the Albany. I will

explain everything. Don't tell your husband—he is still in grave danger.

Arturo

RUBINA GASPED and clutched it to her chest.

"Is everything all right?" Simmons asked.

"It's fine." Rubina forced a smile on her face. "I need to visit Gemma and Lily. Gemma isn't feeling well enough for travel."

"Would you like me to have the carriage brought around?"

"No need. I think I will walk. I could use the fresh air, and it's not too far away. Tell Noah, if he should return before I do, I look forward to dinner this evening. He said he had a something to talk to me about."

"Very well, Your Grace." He bowed and left the room.

Rubina folded up Arturo's note and rushed out of the room. She didn't even stop to grab her pelisse. There was no time. Paolo had her brother. She needed to know what happened. The sooner she reached Arturo the quicker she would get the information she needed.

When she exited the townhouse she ran into Lily

and almost knocked her down the steps. Gemma blocked her fall.

"Where are you off to in a hurry?" Lily asked.

Drat. There went her excuse to leave the house. Simmons would question why Gemma was visiting when Rubina was supposedly off to see her.

"I need to get to the Albany." She might as well go for some version of the truth. "Damian needs me."

"Is he ill?" Gemma asked. "We can come with you."

That was a very bad idea.

"No." Rubina shook her head. "I don't think he would be up for company."

"Nonsense," Lily interrupted her. "We can't let you travel on your own. It wouldn't be right. We will escort you over there."

Gemma nibbled on her lip. "Noah wouldn't like it. He's rather protective of you since, you know—you're not dead as he believed you to be."

There was no getting out of it. She'd have to tell them the truth. They were not going to leave her alone and Damian was in trouble. Rubina sighed and handed the note to Lily.

"Read that and let's get moving. This very well could be life and death."

Lily opened the note and frowned. "Who is Paolo, and why does he have Damian?"

"It's a long story?"

"Why don't you start with Arturo and why he sent you this note." Lily waved the missive in front of her.

Rubina nodded. "I will tell you everything, but please, we need to get to the Albany, so follow me."

Gemma raised her hand. "Why don't we take my carriage? It would save time and we can talk in comfort."

Rubina's gaze flew to the carriage. Gemma did have a point. The only reason she hadn't ordered her own was because it would take too long. Having one already available though...

"Yes, that's a good idea." Rubina headed to the carriage and hopped inside. Gemma and Lily followed her. "To answer one of your questions... Arturo is one of Damian's employees—and I owe him my life."

Lily and Gemma looked at each other and then back to Rubina. "I think we need more details."

Rubina sighed. "When I left Noah, I fully intended to come home to him. I never wanted to leave him."

"Go on," Lily encouraged.

"I was set to board a ship to Florence to visit my father. Noah and I had an argument…"

Rubina held back tears. Her voice cracked as she spoke.

"I know it's hard," Gemma said in a soft voice. "But it will help tell us everything. It must be hard keeping all your secrets buried inside."

Rubina wiped her eyes. "Paolo had his men grab me before I got on board. He took me to his home in Sicily and kept me captive there…" She paused and stared off in space. "He wanted me, but I'd refused him. I married Noah and never regretted that decision. He's the only man I've ever loved." She stared at Gemma and Lily. "Arturo rescued me and took me to my brother's ship. It was there I found out how truly evil Paolo is and that Noah was going to marry another woman. I had to return."

"So all this time…" Gemma's voice trailed off.

"I lived in a locked room, held prisoner by a mad man."

"Now he has your brother?" Lily's voice hardened. "That is wrong."

"I have to find a way to save Damian." Rubina struggled to control her emotions. She straightened her spine and said with conviction, "But above all, Paolo must die."

"Rubina…" Gemma's voice trailed off.

"No. Don't tell me it will be a black stain on my soul. Allowing him to live would be an error of the greatest multitude. He will never stop coming after me and those I love. The only way to ensure that we are all safe is for him to cease to be. That man belongs in hell, and I will send him there."

"We will help you," Lily blurted out.

Gemma's gaze flew to hers. "Are you sure?"

"Yes. You saw how Noah was when he believed Rubina died. For that alone, this man must pay."

Gemma turned toward Rubina and nodded. "She's right, but we must at least try to be careful. Liam will be so mad if something happens…"

Lily's lips curved into a gamine smile. "My brother will get over it."

"I don't think this is a good idea. You should both drop me off at the Albany and return home. I'd never forgive myself if something happened to you to." Rubina wanted them all safe.

"Too late." Lily said and jumped out of the carriage when it came to a stop. "Meet you inside."

"Lily has always been rather—impetuous," Gemma offered.

"I know." Rubina sighed. "I suppose we should follow her."

The both got out of the carriage and gasped as someone grabbed a hold of them. Lily was being held by a burly man with black curly hair and mean eyes.

"You weren't supposed to bring friends, *la mia bellezza*." Paolo cooed in her ear. "You're as beautiful as I remember. You were a bad girl though, running off with that man. I'll have to make you pay for that."

She was not his beauty.

Rubina spit in his face. "What have you done with my brother?"

"He's safe—for now." He wiped his face. "If you do as I tell you, I may even allow him to live."

"Let Gemma and Lily go," Rubina demanded. "They mean nothing to you."

He shook his head. "I'm afraid I can't do that. They are very much a part of this now. You shouldn't have brought them if you were concerned for their safety. They can keep you company for a while…"

"Then what?" Rubina was almost afraid to ask.

"Depends on their attitude." He laughed evilly. "If they are cooperative, I might let my men have a go at them… If not, well, they can be easily disposed of."

Bile rose in her throat. This was all her fault. How could she have allowed this to happen. Maybe there was still hope. If Arturo was in her brother's rooms... Her gaze flew to the entrance of the Albany.

"If you're wondering about Arturo, he isn't going to come and save you."

Had he read her mind? "How can you be so certain?"

"Because he didn't send you that note, *cara*." He caressed her cheek with the back of his hand. "It was all a ruse to get you out of the house. I'm afraid Arturo is very much dead."

"No..."

"He had to pay for his insolence. If not for his actions, you'd still be where you belong."

Lily bit the man's finger that held her. "Ouch, you bitch."

"You won't get away with this. Our husbands will hunt you down and kill you like the rabid dog you are."

Paolo laughed. "Such fire. Maybe I will keep you for myself after all."

Lily struggled to get free.

"Restrain the spitfire and put her in the carriage." He then gestured toward Gemma. "Put her in there too and take care of the men that were following them. Make sure they don't live to tell tales."

Paolo dragged Rubina along with him, separating her from Gemma and Lily.

"Where are you taking me?"

"Those two have a few lessons to learn." He grinned. "You, my dear, have a much harsher one to finally grasp. We are going to arrive at our destination separate from your friends."

"Please, let them go."

She had to try one last time. Her heart was breaking into pieces. If she could save them…

"I said no. They are part of the price you need to pay for leaving me."

Rubina grimaced. Paolo had grown crazier since the last time she'd seen him.

"I am not yours to keep."

"You are," he bellowed. "You will finally understand that you belong to me."

"I will never be yours." Rubina elbowed him in his side. She attempted to wrench herself free, but it was a futile endeavor.

"Yes. You are mine." He pulled her into his arms. "Look at me."

Rubina let her gaze fall down. She didn't want to look into his fanatical eyes. A huge part of her was afraid of what she might see in them.

"I said look at me," he demanded, lifting her chin.

"That's better. I want you to know who it is that holds you. Who will always hold you from this point on."

Paolo leaned down and touched his lips to hers. Rubina fought him, but he held on tight. He forced her mouth open and pushed his tongue inside of her mouth. Rubina bit it as hard as she could until she tasted blood.

"You bitch" He slapped her face. "That's one more thing you will pay for. I am no longer going to be a gentleman with you. I mean to have you tonight. Finally, you will belong to me in every way."

Rubina held back a shudder—barely. She had to do something to save herself, and those she loved. The idea of Paolo... No, she refused to even picture the heinous things he had planned.

Paolo shoved her into a nearby carriage and tapped the roof. Wherever he was taking her...they were well on their way. She would have to get inside his head a little bit and make him start to doubt this foolhardy plan of his.

She grinned, evilly. "When will you understand that there is not a chance in hell of you ever having me in any way. My heart, body, and soul belong to my husband. When he finds me—and he will find me, Paolo—you will finally burn in the fires of hell for what you have done to us."

Noah said he would always come for her. So if she couldn't find a way to save herself, her only hope was that her husband would tear the world apart looking for her.

Not to mention, Liam was as much of an alpha male as Noah. They wouldn't allow their wives to be held hostage by a mad man. Rubina didn't know Rand well…but she did know Lily. That woman wouldn't go for a weak man. There would be a reckoning.

Rubina couldn't wait to see Paolo torn to shreds.

"That is where you are wrong." Paolo's grin sent fear into her heart. "Soon your husband will be as dead as I originally claimed. I am leaving nothing to chance this time."

Bloody hell…he had to be lying. Right?

Now Rubina had one more thing to stress about. Paolo would not win.

Even if she had to take her last breath to see him dead—he would go to hell where he belonged.

CHAPTER SEVENTEEN

*N*oah hopped the steps two at a time and swung open the door to his townhouse.

"Rubina," he bellowed.

He was met with complete silence.

Bloody hell. Where was his wife?

"Her Grace went to visit Lady Marsden." Simmons entered the foyer. "She left at the beginning of the hour. She bade me to tell you she was looking forward to dinner this evening."

Noah frowned.

"We could just get back in the carriage and go to see her." Liam stood in the open doorway. "Luckily my townhouse isn't too far from yours. It wouldn't take long to get there."

Liam did have a point. Did he really want to have it out with Rubina in front of Gemma—and possibly Lily? That wasn't a good idea at all. It would put her even more on the defensive.

"No," he shook his head. "I can be patient a little while longer. I'm sure she's perfectly safe at your place."

"Why are you standing in an open doorway?" Rand stood behind Liam. "Is Lily inside? I need her to come back to Marsden house. William is driving the staff mad. When he gets like this, the only one that can subdue him is her."

Liam frowned. "Why would Lily be here?"

"Because she came with Gemma to visit Rubina." Rand rolled his eyes. "Lily had this harebrained idea Rubina needed cheering up about something."

A sick feeling took root in Noah's gut. None of the ladies were inside...

"Lily and Gemma are not here." Noah's hand shook. "Rubina isn't here either."

Liam's normally dark complexion paled. "You don't think..."

"Did someone fail to send me an invitation to this party?"

They all turned to see Marcus stumble toward

the entrance of the town house. He winced with each step, but he no longer held on to his side.

"Why in tarnation are you here?" Noah asked.

"One of my men managed to get away…" He paused and shook his head. "The details don't matter. I had to let you know d'Sordillo has your wife and the other two women traveling with her."

Liam cursed and punched the door. "That evil bastard has my wife."

"Someone want to fill me in?" Rand glanced back and forth between all three men. "Who took them?"

None of them volunteered the information.

Noah clenched his jaw struggling to get a hold of his emotions. This was all his worst fears wrapped neatly into one nightmarish package. "I need the location of his hidey hole."

"I'm coming with you," Liam demanded.

"I didn't expect you would want to stay behind."

Rand started to wave his hands. "Hello? Someone better start telling me what is going on before I start hitting one of you to get it."

Marcus shook his head. "I will have to take you there. The place is too secluded to give you directions."

Noah nodded. "Well, as luck would have it Liam's carriage is still available. I suggest we all get inside and go rescue our wives from a man who has unmistakably lost his mind."

Rand folded his arms across his chest and glared at Noah. "I'm still waiting for you to tell me what the hell has you all fired up."

"Not now, man. We don't have time for this." Liam smacked him on the shoulder. "Get in the bloody carriage, and we can fill you in on the way."

Noah remained silent. He was afraid if he said too much he'd break down and crumble. All the lies and secrets—none of it mattered anymore. His only concern was finding Rubina and bringing her home safely…

"You two whoresons are going to get an earful from me on the way to wherever we are headed to retrieve the women." Rand glared at them both before he hopped inside the carriage.

Noah couldn't fault the man. He'd be cussing too. Hell, he wanted to do a lot more than that. He wanted to pummel something until it was torn to shreds.

Paolo would make a good target for all that pent up angst.

Marcus rattled off directions to the driver and hopped inside the carriage with them.

"Start talking," Rand demanded. "What in the dickens is happening to our wives?"

Noah took a deep breath and steeled himself for Rand's displeasure. "Rubina was kidnapped."

"I gathered that," Rand interrupted him. "Along with Gemma and Lily. Who would do that?"

"That was what I was trying to tell you." Noah shook his head. "This dates back to when Rubina went missing the first time."

If only he'd known she'd been held captive for so many years. She must have lost faith in him. No wonder she wanted to leave him. Why would she want a husband who didn't protect her? Noah had been set to reprimand her for keeping it all a secret. The reasons why didn't matter anymore. She could keep any bloody thing she wanted to herself—as long as she was safe. He loved her too much to try to cage her in. It was time he let her be as free as she wanted.

Rand nodded. "I remember you believed she died, but she just came home recently. Did she tell you what happened to her?"

If only she had...

"No." Rand frowned. Noah continued, "I hired Marcus here to look into the matter. He was injured gathering the information for me and explained all the details earlier. When we arrived at my town-house, the women were already missing."

"I suppose that is where I come in," Marcus inter-rupted. "My men were keeping an eye on the duchess. All I know for sure is they got in Lady Marsden's carriage and went to visit Her Grace's brother. Outside of the Albany, they were snatched. Duca d'Sordillo took Rubina, and the other two were taken in a different carriage."

Liam's mouth fell open. He closed it and clenched his jaw. Then after a few more seconds said, "Lily and Gemma were taken to a separate location?"

"I don't even know if Rubina is being taken to where we are headed. This is the only place that I know they could've been taken. It's a starting point."

Bollocks… What a bloody mess this was all turning into.

"How long until we arrive?" Rand asked quietly.

Noah was getting a little worried about the man. He had grown silent with each bit of information they departed on him. It appeared as if his sole focus was on what needed to be done. At least one of them remained calm and collected. It would come in handy when they reached their destination.

"We're not far behind them." Marcus gestured toward Noah. "Shortly after you left, my man stumbled in. As luck would have it, the doctor got two for the price of one. He was still patching him up when I left." He turned to Rand. "To answer your question, we should arrive soon. It isn't far outside of the city —it's well hidden."

They all kept their thoughts to themselves from that point on. Each man focused on their own concerns. Noah ran his hands over his face. This was his fault. He should have demanded answers from Rubina sooner. If he had... His jaw tightened. Noah hit the side of the carriage with his hand.

"Easy now. That's not going to solve anything," Liam reminded him.

Noah glared. "Like hitting the door helped you."

"Fair enough." He frowned. "Now isn't the time for anger. We need to remain as calm as possible. After they are safe, we can unleash it on the bastard that took them."

"I'm going to rip him to pieces."

They all focused on Rand—each man's mouth hung open in surprise. He'd been so quiet and calm. His statement was unexpected.

"I think you might have to stand in line and wait your turn." Liam shook his head. "It's always the quiet ones that surprise you."

The carriage came to a halt.

Noah stared at each man and nodded. "It's time."

They all got out and made their way to the place Paolo stashed the women—or at least where they hoped he had. If they were in another location…

Noah wouldn't think about it. They had to be inside.

"Do you know anything about this place?" Noah asked Marcus.

He shook his head. "Not much. There are guards at each entrance. There are at least six men inside. At the top of the hour patrols go out and do a perimeter check."

"No pressure at all…" Liam shook his head. "The good news is that it's past their hourly checkpoint. If we can get past a couple of the guards at the back entrance, we might be able to break in and rescue the women without too much fuss."

It was probably the best chance they were going to get to make it happen.

"Once we're inside, we will split up and search. Liam, come with me and Rand go with Marcus." He nodded to each man. "Let's do this."

They sneaked their way across the lawn. Two men patrolled the perimeter. Noah gestured to Liam and he nodded. They each circled around to deal with them and efficiently knocked out the two guards. One hurdle down, many more to go, until the women were safe. They remained as silent as possible as they entered the house.

It was time to divide and conquer, Noah looked toward the stairs gesturing to Liam to follow him. Rand and Marcus went left down the first hall. Liam and Noah made their way to the second story. They moved their way down the hallway at a slow pace. Careful to not make any noise and check each room they passed. A shrill voice filled his ears and he stopped to listen. Noah heard shouting as he crept toward a door at the end of the path.

"I told you." A woman's laugh filled the room. "You didn't listen to me."

"Cara," the male voice coaxed. "Put the pistol down. You don't really want to shoot me."

"I assure you," the woman said with conviction. "Not only do I want to, but I will."

Rubina…

Noah pushed open the door and found his wife holding a pistol in her hands. Her golden blonde hair fell down her back in waves. Her eyes were the color of melted silver.

"Don't be so hasty, Ruby dear. If you kill me, you will never find your brother."

Rubina raised the pistol higher, aiming for

Paolo's head. "You implied he's already dead. Now you want to change your story?"

"I may have exaggerated a bit." His grin was filled with menace. "He was a thorn in my side. I had to take him or he'd have caused problems. He could be alive." Paolo shrugged. "He could be dead. I don't know for sure. If you put the gun down, I can tell you how to find out for certain."

Her hand shook. "I don't believe you."

"You need to stop her," Liam said. "Killing him would be a mistake, at least for now. Lily and Gemma are still unaccounted for. We can always end him later."

"I know," Noah agreed.

He eased his way inside, getting a little closer to Rubina. He had to get the gun from her before she did something she would regret. Taking person's life, even someone as evil as Paolo, would haunt her.

"Ruby?" Noah approached her. "Give me the gun. You don't want to kill him."

She shook her head. "I do. You don't know what he's put me through. He needs to die."

A tear fell from the corner of her eye and trailed down her cheek.

"Rubina," Liam's voice was filled with panic. "Where are Gemma and Lily?"

She shook her head. "I don't know…"

"Well, I do have some use left then." The man laughed with malevolence. "You may not care for Damian, but those two women are important enough to stay my execution."

"There is no reason to allow you to keep breathing. We will find Gemma and Lily without your help." Rubina held the gun up higher. "I am going to send you to hell today, Paolo."

Liam paled at her words. His hand raised as if itching to take the gun away from Rubina. His jerky movements raised Noah's anxiety. He needed a new task before he tried to wrestle Rubina for control of the gun. Liam's concern for Gemma was warring with his good sense.

"Liam, go help Rand and Marcus search the rest of the house. I will take care of this." Noah turned to Rubina. "Please, Ruby. Give it to me."

Liam stilled and stared at Noah. He didn't want to leave. Noah understood. If it were his wife, he'd want more information too. Him being in the room wasn't helping though. He could go do something productive, such as actually trying to find the women. Perhaps they were still inside, and he could aid them in exiting the premises. After several seconds, he nodded and left. Noah breathed

DAWN BROWER

a sigh of relief. Only one more pressing problem to get through before he could let go of his own anxiety.

Rubina's hand shook. If he didn't take the pistol from her soon, she might hurt herself.

Noah eased over to her side and wrapped his hand around hers. The hilt of the pistol was encased in both of their hands. "Let me do it."

She shook her head. "No. It's my vengeance to take." Rubina shook his hand free of hers. They were both distracted and took their eyes off of their enemy for a few precious seconds.

Paolo rushed forward. Rubina flinched, causing her to squeeze the trigger. A loud boom filled the room as the gun went off.

The look of shock on the man's face—he really believed he'd make it out of the situation alive. His body crumpled and hit the floor with a loud thump. Rubina's hand shook and the pistol fell from her hand, landing on the hard surface with a sharp thud. Tears fell in a rush from her eyes.

"Is he really dead?"

Noah only had eyes for his wife. He pulled her into his arms and held her as tight as he could. "I've never been so scared in my life. Don't do that to me ever again."

"I'm so sorry." Her tears fell harder with each breath she took. "Please forgive me."

"Shhh." He kept his voice as soothing as possible. Noah reined in his emotions. Rubina needed him to be strong. "No one will hurt you I won't let them."

It was a promise he intended to keep.

"I love you," Rubina whispered. "I never stopped."

"I know," he reassured her.

A part of him had always known. It had taken him a little while to get over his anger. A love like theirs didn't just go away. They were meant to be together forever, and now they wouldn't have anything to stand in their way.

"There is something else." She stared up into his eyes. "I wanted to tell you everything, but I was so afraid. There is nothing preventing me now."

Noah ran his fingers through her hair relishing in the silkiness of her curls. "You can tell me anything. Don't ever feel like you need to keep secrets from me. Nothing you could say would ever change how I feel about you."

He wiped the tears from her eyes. A small smile formed on her face.

"This is good news."

"You're carrying our child," he finished for her.

She glanced up with surprise. "You knew?"

He laughed. For the first time, his heart didn't constrict with pain—instead only joy filled it.

"I suspected." He kissed her lips lightly.

She bit her lip. "Are you happy?"

"More than words can say." He wrapped his arms around her once again. "But it's not all settled. Lily and Gemma need to be found."

"All taken care of." Marcus stepped into the room. "They are headed toward the carriage to go home with their husbands."

"How are we going to get back?"

"Paolo took Gemma's carriage. It's probably still here," Rubina explained.

"Her Grace is correct." He nodded. "I will drive it back since the driver didn't make it here with it."

Marcus left to go prepare the carriage for their journey.

Noah smiled. "Everything worked out how it was supposed to."

Rubina frowned. "Not entirely. We still don't know what happened to Damian."

He could see the concern in her eyes. She'd been so brave facing down Paolo. Her brother meant so much to her. How could he make it better? Damian could still be alive. Paolo never confirmed one way or the other.

"We will find him."

"I don't know if that is possible." She nibbled on her bottom lip. "The duca was an evil man. I shudder to think what he did to my brother. Perhaps death would be kinder."

Noah feared Rubina would never be able to fully recover from the atrocities she endured. "I will have Marcus investigate. If anyone can locate your brother, he can. Try not to worry overmuch. We will have answers. It might just take a while to get them."

Once they found Damian, everything would be right in their world. Rubina's happiness was all that mattered to him. They had a life to build together. The only blight on that was Damian's predicament.

"Yes, *caro*." Rubina cupped his cheek in the palm of her hand. A hint of sadness still lingered in her eyes. "Are you ready to go home?"

"I'm already home." He kissed her cheek. "My home is wherever you are. But yes, let's leave this place behind us and go somewhere inherently more pleasant."

*R*ubina caressed his cheek. It was soft and beautiful. He was the most beautiful child in all of creation. Perhaps all mothers believed that of their children, but she couldn't stop looking at him.

It gave her a small amount of joy through a difficult time. Knowing her son was alive and well while her brother...

She didn't want to think about Damian. They had been grieving him for months. There seemed to be no reason to believe Paolo hadn't murdered him. Throughout her entire pregnancy they had searched for any sign he might be alive. Whatever Paolo had done... They couldn't find any answers. When Lucien was born, they were forced to give up the search. The family went into mourning. Now that her son was a year old, it was time to let her brother go. They had much to live for.

"Are you staring at Lucien again?" Noah entered the nursery. "Let the poor boy nap."

She pouted. "But he is so lovely when he's sleeping. When he's awake, he often gets in touch with his impish side."

Noah leaned downed and gave her a quick kiss on the lips. "This surprises you? The Marsden twins are his playmates."

"You make it sound as if Alexander and Andrew have the ear of the devil himself."

"No, but I don't know how Liam and Gemma keep up with them. Once they started walking…"

Rubina laughed. "They are adorable."

"Come with me," he urged. "I have a surprise for you."

Rubina looked down one last time at her son. He had his father's dark brown hair and her silver eyes. He was the perfect mixture of both of them. It was hard to believe he was going to be a year old in less than a week.

"What do you have for me?" She turned toward her husband. "You give me the best gifts."

The best one being their son…

He led her down the hall to her bedroom—turned dressing room. She never slept in it. Not when she could sleep encased in her husband's loving arms.

"Why are we here?" She asked.

"Go inside."

She stared at him, puzzled, but did as he bid.

Inside, lying on top of her bed, was one of the most beautiful gowns she'd ever seen. It was pure white with silver lace embellishments. Tiny seed pearls were sewn into the bodice and shined against the lace.

"What is this?"

He grinned. "Do you remember our two week deal?"

Rubina nodded. It had been when he believed he needed to court her again. Foolish man—she never stopped loving him.

"I had this elaborate plan. It all fell apart—well, you know why. I put it on hold, but I think today is a good time to see it through."

He pulled a ring out of his pocket and held it before her. It was a ruby flanked by diamonds on each side.

"Noah?"

"Will you marry me again?" He lifted her hand

and kissed it. "I promise to love you forever. I even had it engraved inside. I know that Paolo took your wedding ring—I want you to wear this one as a symbol of how much I will always love you."

Rubina took the ring from him and looked inside. Ruby, my heart beats for you—Noah

Tears fell from her eyes.

"So, is that a yes?"

She rushed into his arms and kissed him. "Did you think I'd be foolish enough to say no?"

Noah grinned. "Ruby, love—life wouldn't be interesting if you became predictable."

"This is true." She laughed.

"A maid will be up in a minute to help you put on your new gown."

"Today?" She asked surprised.

"Did you think I'd wait more than a few moments to make you mine?" He raised an eyebrow. "I can't let the world believe, even for a second, that you are not my wife."

Rubina laughed. "We wouldn't want that."

It didn't matter that they were already married. This was the fresh started that had been denied to them. This was one thing she would do over and over again if it kept their love where it belonged.

Noah left the room and allowed her time to change.

When she came down the stairs, she had to choke back tears. Her father stood at the bottom to escort her to her groom.

"Papa." She hugged him. "How long have you known about this?"

He cupped her cheeks in the palm of his hands and kissed her forehead. "Long enough to sail across the ocean to be here with you."

"Thank you."

"I wouldn't be anywhere else." His eyes were full of warmth as he looked down at her. "You're my only daughter, and I thank God that you are still with us."

Noah stood next to a vicar, waiting for Rubina to join him. Their friends and family all sat in chairs, watching for her arrival. Lily and Rand had even made another trip from America to attend. Her eyes narrowed into tiny slits at one of the guests—Pearla Montgomery. What was she doing there? Rubina hadn't seen her since that fateful day she'd interrupted her wedding to Noah. She sat next to Gemma and Liam. Maybe this was some torturous closure she was putting herself through. Rubina didn't care. She could be generous after all—she had Noah.

Maybe if Pearla was lucky enough, she would find someone as equally wonderful. It was the least she could wish for. The woman had lost a wonderful man—she deserved to move on and find her own happiness.

They all turned to see her walk toward her husband.

This was so very different than the wedding she interrupted.

It was all about her and Noah.

Her husband's smile grew wider with each step she took toward him.

She moved forward to meet him. "Hello, *caro.*"

"I was beginning to think I'd have to come find you."

Rubina smiled. "You will never have to come find me ever again. I will always be right here by your side..."

They said their vows. Emotions welled up inside her as she spoke them. Hearing them reaffirmed everything she wanted with Noah. They had been through so much. Going through the ceremony again helped them take back what belonged to them. Nothing would separate them again. They had their whole lives to look forward to.

"You may now kiss your bride."

Noah stared down into her eyes. "You don't have to tell me twice."

"Pardon me for interrupting—I always did show up late for important events."

Noah and Rubina glanced across the room. A gasp of surprise fell from Rubina's lips. Her brother strutted in—as if he didn't have a care in the world. Never mind they believed him dead. This must be how her family felt when they thought she'd died. His hair was a little longer than she remembered. It fell to his shoulders in long black waves, but his silver eyes held something she couldn't identify. He'd changed. Rubina didn't know what it was, but it looked good on him.

Rubina ran to him and hugged him tight. "I'm so glad to see you. Where the bloody hell have you been all this time?"

Damian hugged her tight in his embrace. He kissed the top of her head.

"Easy now, Rue." He eased back. "I rather like breathing."

"Are you going to answer my question?" She raised an eyebrow.

"I will explain it all at another time." He scanned the guests. "I came for another reason."

Rubina pursed her lips in displeasure. She was

happy to see her brother but... She stopped and looked at him. Then she turned in the direction that held him riveted.

Pearla stood up. Her blue eyes shot daggers at Damian. Her hand flew to her chest; her mouth hung open with shock. She shook her head several times as if not believing what she saw in front of her. Rubina could relate to what she appeared to be going through.

She turned to her brother and asked, "Do you two know each other?"

"I think a man would know his wife when he sees her." Damian's eyes never left Pearla.

Rubina stared back and forth between them. Even more questions entered her mind. When had these two met? All she knew about Pearla was she was gone for more than a year nursing a broken heart—who could blame her? She'd have been devastated if she'd lost Noah to another woman too.

"I am not your wife," Pearla said with disdain.

Pearla pushed her way past everyone. She left the house in a huff, with Damian not far behind her. Rubina shook her head. It was their mess to straighten. They would work it out—or wouldn't. She just hoped her brother found happiness. He could explain what happened when he settled things with Pearla. Rubina liked to think she learned patience over the past several years. Damian deserved happiness, and if that was with Pearla she wouldn't stand in the way.

Liam strolled over to stand next to her. "I will say one thing about you and weddings—never a dull moment."

He laughed and walked away.

Blasted man did have a point. Although, their first wedding was uneventful...

"Don't listen to my brother," Lily interrupted. "This was the best wedding ever. Think of the stories you can tell you children. Noah's an honorary Marsden, you know. So he should have a tale like the rest of us."

"What do you mean?" Rubina asked.

Noah laughed. "The bedtime story your parents told you two?"

"Yes." Lily nodded excitedly. "I know, yours can start with: once upon a time, a woman objected to a wedding..."

Rubina and Noah laughed. It wasn't how they actually began, but it did tell how they found each other again. Perhaps this was a tradition she could get behind.

EXCERPT: A DISCARDED PEARL

A MARSDEN ROMANCE BOOK FIVE

DAWN BROWER

CHAPTER ONE

*H*eat filled her cheeks as she rushed across the dock toward the ship she'd secured passage on. Pearla Montgomery wanted as much distance between her and England as she could possibly get. Had anyone ever experienced such monumental embarrassment?

"No. That honor only goes to me," she muttered under her breath.

She had been so close to marrying Noah St. John, the Duke of Huntly. She'd fallen in love with him the moment she saw him. The hurt spilling out of his chocolate brown eyes...all she wanted to do was wrap him up in her arms and ease the pain away. Noah didn't or, to be more accurate, *couldn't* love her. She knew that, but she hoped in time he would at least come to care for her.

Unfortunately, his not-so-dead wife had crashed their wedding. *Had it only been that morning?* Rubina had waltzed into the church without a by-your-leave. Not that the woman needed permission. Her husband had been about to marry another woman. In her position, Pearla would have done the same. If only she'd come home sooner and prevented the resulting embarrassment. For that alone, Pearla resented her intrusion.

No one had known Rubina lived. Noah believed he lost her to a watery gave when a ship she'd been sailing on capsized in a storm. Pearla believed if he'd been aware Rubina was alive he'd have searched for her. The duke hadn't said much about his wife, but it was clear he loved her. The tone in his voice changed whenever he said her name. When she'd appeared at the church, it had become clear the duchess's resurrection was the end of Pearla's relationship with Noah. It was a combination of sadness and happiness that filled her heart at the sight of Rubina. She was ecstatic for him, and morose that she had to relinquish the connection they'd shared. Rubina was the woman he loved; Pearla was the usurper in their relationship.

"Just my luck." Pearla sighed and marched toward the ship.

She'd rushed home, demanded her maid to remove her wedding attire, and ordered her trunks packed for a different trip. If she never laid eyes on the bloody dress ever again, it'd be too soon. At the day's start, she'd thought she would be moving into Noah's townhouse. The staff had been given instructions to send the trunks to his home later in the day. Pearla was no longer going to be his duchess, and never would be. Not that she wanted the title; it'd been the man she craved. Sadly, she had to let go of that desire. Now, here she was, hours later, preparing to embark on an alternate excursion. The sun would be setting on all her hopes and dreams in a few hours. This was a day she'd not soon forget, but not for the reasons she originally thought.

"Can I help you, missy?"

Pearla turned and held in a breath. She cringed at the sight of the burly man before her. His demeanor was menacing, and he was covered in dirt and grime. By the smell of him he'd not deigned to bathe in several days—perhaps weeks. He stood near the gangway to board the ship, blocking her path. She lifted her chin and glared at him as haughtily as she could manage.

"I am Miss Pearla Montgomery. I have passage on this ship."

"Do you now?" His eyes leered across her bosom. "Why don't you wait here while I go and find the Captain."

It took everything she had to not visibly shake under his lewd gaze. This was just a means to an end. It wouldn't do to stay in England and watch Noah being blissfully happy with his wife. No one expected Pearla to stay and witness their reunion. Her best friend, Gemma Marsden supported her decision. She was happy for Noah. Truly, she was.

However, she wasn't in the least joyful at her own circumstances. Running away from the problems life had thrown at her wasn't an ideal situation. Everything she'd done since her wedding had ended in failure screamed of desperation. It was a sad fact. She'd loved a man who wasn't available. If only she'd known before she'd suffered the shame of loving him. Losing him and what they could have had... She shook her head and cleared her thoughts. Noah wasn't hers. That unfortunate outcome was for the best. Marriage hadn't been in her plans until he waltzed into her life. It was time to do what she'd originally intended. Travel the world and see what it had to offer. The morning's disaster prompted what should have been her path all along.

"Miss Montgomery?"

Pearla's gaze shot upward and landed on a tall man with a scruffy beard. "Yes."

"My bosun tells me you've secured passage aboard my ship."

She played with her lip between her teeth. There better not be some mistake. It would be awful if she'd been played a fool and some thief, under the guise of booking her passage, stole her funds. She had to be on this ship. "I spoke to someone named Paolo about an hour ago."

He narrowed his eyes and studied her. He nodded. "I am Captain Blythe. I do recall Paolo saying we would have a couple passengers. Please, follow me."

A couple of passengers? She didn't bring a lady's maid. The idea of having anyone with her...made her uneasy. It was not something she wanted to deal with. As far as she was concerned, she didn't have a reputation to salvage. Why put up with someone that would only get in her way. Still, she couldn't help wondering who else was supposed to board the ship. She hoped the captain didn't expect them to share a cabin. Pearla wanted to be alone, and having a cabin mate would be too annoying.

The captain led her below deck to a small room with one narrow bunk. She breathed a sigh of relief. With only one bunk, surely that meant she would be alone as she wished.

"Do you have trunks that needed to be brought aboard the ship?"

The captain's words snapped her out of her own mind. "Yes. They are in my carriage. Do you have someone that can retrieve them? If not, I can have the footmen bring them aboard."

He nodded. "I will have my men secure them below deck."

Pearla set her valise and reticule on the bunk. The only things she expected to have on the long journey were inside her traveling bags. The rest she'd worry over later. She didn't even have any idea where this particular ship was heading. It had the only thing she required when looking for passage: it left immediately.

"Captain," the burly man from earlier interrupted. "Our other passenger has arrived."

The captain turned toward him and said, "Perfect. Then we can set sail as soon as the anchor is hoisted."

The man stared lewdly at Pearla. She gulped back unease that pooled at the bottom of her stomach. She would lock her door after they left. The way the man looked at her made her skin crawl.

"Are you wishing me to keep you company?" The disgusting man licked his lips suggestively. Pearla lifted her hand and held a finger under her nose. The captain needed to control his men better. This one in particular needed to understand his place better.

Pearla shook her head and stumbled back into the room. "No. I'm fine. Honestly. Perhaps you should help with the new passenger." She gestured toward the captain.

"Leave the young lady alone, Perry," the captain ordered. "She's right. I do need your help with our new guest. Besides, the boss gave express instructions to make sure we keep Miss Montgomery safe on her journey."

Perry? She wrinkled her nose. Even his name was distasteful. The captain's smile made her feel even more uneasy. Paolo must be his boss. He did seem overly concerned for her welfare. Maybe she had lucked out in that regard. She certainly hoped so because she didn't like how Perry was ogling her. He smacked his lips as if anticipating his favorite sweet treat would touch his tongue. It wasn't something she particularly liked seeing. He was a combination of scary and disgusting. Did he believe in bathing at all? She wanted to cover her nose and mouth again. It took every ounce of etiquette instilled in her to refrain from doing so. He could leave the cabin and his offending odor would still linger.

"Too bad. We could have had some fun, you and I." He wiggled his eyebrows. "Let me know if you be changing your mind."

"While I appreciate your, um…" She paused, considered her words, "offer, I must decline."

"We will leave you to make yourself comfortable." The captain turned to leave. "Please stay in your cabin for now. You will be in the way as we set sail. I will let you know when it's safe to come on deck."

Pearla nodded. She didn't have a problem with the request. She was more than happy to wallow in self pity in her cabin. It would give her time to properly grieve what she lost. The man of her dreams… How does a woman get over that?

The captain closed the door with a *click*. A key turned in the lock. *What the hell?* She said she would stay in the cabin. Why would the captain lock her inside? She walked over to the door and yanked at the door knob, hoping she'd been wrong. Unfortunately, she wasn't. The damned man had made it impossible for her to leave.

That uneasy feeling turned into angry knots pounding through her whole body. Her breathing became frantic. There was very little light in the cabin. The small porthole only allowed a tiny stream of sunlight into the room. Was she to suffer in the dark? She scanned the room to see if perhaps there was a lantern she could light. Nothing.

She stormed back to the door and pounded on it with her fists. "Let me out. Let me out now. I can't breathe."

No one came to her rescue. She was truly stuck. What had she gotten herself into?

Pearla crumpled against the wall underneath the porthole. Letting the sun bathe her in what little light the hole allowed. She let her face drop into her palms as tears fell from her eyes. In everything that happened, she hadn't allowed herself the time to cry. She'd lost so much, and apparently she was about to lose much more before the day was done. It served her right for acting so foolhardy.

Stupid. Stupid. Stupid.

Pearla wasn't sure how much time passed as she gave into her misery, but it seemed like ages. She glanced at the porthole. There was still some sunlight, so night hadn't fallen yet. When she arrived on the dock it had been early evening. The setting sun gave her something to work with time-wise. With the onset of warm weather, they gained more daylight hours, which meant she'd been locked in the cabin at least a couple hours. The door creaked open, and Pearla shot to her feet. Finally, someone was coming to let her out. They had heard her. *Thank God.*

A body was shoved inside. Whoever it was tumbled to the ground with a loud *thud.* Just as fast as the door opened, it was closed again. She hopped over the unconscious figure and pounded on the door.

"You can't leave him in here with me. Come back," she shouted. "There isn't room enough for one person, let alone two."

They ignored her. Bloody rotten bastards, the lot of them. She would get even with them for being so inconsiderate. Her fists clenched tight against her side as her cheeks flushed with heat. It might take time, but they would regret treating her like common baggage.

A small groan filled the silence. Perhaps she should check on her cabin mate. Who knows what they did to the poor soul. Pearla kneeled down beside him and rolled him over onto his back. Sunlight spilled across his face, and she sucked in a breath. He had an angry knot swelling across his forehead, but everything else about him was perfect. Inky black hair curled around his shoulder, and his face was almost too pretty to be considered hand-some. She brushed back his hair to get a better look at his injuries. He moaned with her ministrations. His eyes flew open and she once again had the breath knocked out of her. His eyes were so beauti-ful. They were a silver gray that sparkled in the tiny sliver of sunlight sliding through the porthole.

"Who are you?" His voice reminded her of warmed brandy. She'd only consumed the amber liquor once; it'd been enough to know she'd been playing with fire. When this man spoke, his rich timber was similar to that blaze engulfing her from the inside out.

"I should be asking you the same. Why would Captain Blythe toss you in a cabin with me and lock the door?" Pearla shook her head. "What did you do to anger him?"

More importantly what had she done to deserve such ill treatment? At least they didn't shove a malodorous beast into the cabin with her. She'd not have been able to suffer through such torture.

Perry's stench had been rotten. This man almost smelled—nice. If she was forced to share her space with a disreputable man, she could be thankful he wasn't disgusting to gaze upon either. There could be worse fates...

"I had the audacity to disagree with his boss's treatment of my sister." His eyes narrowed. "What did you do to anger him?"

She chewed on her bottom lip. "I don't have any idea."

"What is your name?" he asked.

She shook her head. "You first."

He chuckled and then winced with pain. His hand flew to his forehead. "Fair enough. But have pity on me. I have one bloody hell of a headache."

A smile twitched on her face. "I reserve the right to make life as difficult as possible, sir. I do not know you."

"I think I like you." A cocky grin filled his face. "I am Damian Leone or Conte Leone if you prefer formality." He lifted his hand and traced his fingers across her cheek. "If I get a choice, I'd have you call me Damian."

She raised an eyebrow. "Just Damian?"

"Yes. I have a feeling you and I are going to be spending a lot of time together."

Pearla frowned. "I hope not."

"Does my company displease you that much?"

How was she to explain it had nothing to do with him. This whole mess was not his fault at all. He was quite charming and beautiful to behold. She would have been entranced with him under other circumstances.

"You don't figure into my consideration. I am not familiar with you enough to ascertain if you're likeable or not." She shrugged. "However, I do have to find a way out of this cabin."

"I hate to tell you," he paused and sat up. "But we are not obtaining our freedom for some time. The ship is already sailing out of the harbor."

Pearla cursed and stood. She headed to the porthole and looked outside. The blasted man was right. They were already well on their way. How long had she been in the cabin before they tossed him inside with her? It didn't matter. They were stuck together. She'd have to make the best of it.

"Come, *cara,* and tell me how you found yourself in the company of such disreputable ruffians as those in the employ of Paolo, the Duca d'Sordillo."

"Who?" Pearla sat down on the bunk and huffed out a breath. "I'm not familiar with that name."

"No?" Damian frowned. "That doesn't make

sense. Why would they stick you with me? Tell me your story; maybe I can figure it out once I have all the information. Why are you on this ship?"

"It's kind of a long story." How to explain her failed wedding to a stranger? It wasn't something Pearla looked forward to. She didn't even want to think about it let alone put voice to it.

"I have nothing but time, *cara*." He waved his hand toward the porthole. "I think it's accurate to assume we will be confined to each other's company for the foreseeable future."

"Quit saying that," she demanded.

"What?" he asked, confused.

"I am not your darling."

"Ah." His lips tilted into one of his half-cocky smiles. "You have yet to tell me your name. What else am I to call you?"

Why did he have to have a valid point? More importantly, why did she still refuse to tell him her name? Maybe it was the fantasy of it. There was a certain romanticism to it all. Instead of telling him her name, she told him her story. This was exactly what she needed upon further reflection. A stranger was much easier to talk to then friends. Gemma had meant well, but she could see the pity mixed with concern in her friend's eyes.

"Today was supposed to be my wedding day," she began. When she finished, a loud whistle filled the room, and then he cursed more colorfully than she had.

"Bloody hell, you're Miss Pearla Montgomery." He scrubbed his hands over his face. "It all makes sense now."

"Well, I'm glad you understand what is going on." She crossed her arms across her chest and glared at him. "I sure don't. I'm as confused as ever." Like how the hell did he know who she was? She hadn't mentioned names. All she told him was her fiancé's presumed dead wife interrupted her wedding. The desire to leave England had made her jump on the first ship available. Had rumors spread that fast already?

His next words made her heart almost stop.

"Rubina is my sister."

She had the worst luck of anyone alive. Only she would have the misfortune of being stuck in a room with the brother of the woman who'd ruined her life. Someone out there truly hated her.

Order Here

ABOUT THE AUTHOR

USA TODAY Bestselling author, DAWN BROWER writes both historical and contemporary romance. There are always stories inside her head; she just never thought she could make them come to life. That creativity has finally found an outlet.

Growing up she was the only girl out of six children. She raised two boys into productive young men. There is never a dull moment in her life. Reading books is her favorite hobby and she loves all genres.

She is active on Facebook, Twitter, and Instagram. To follow her or can find more about her check out her website for the pertinent information:

www.authordawnbrower.com

BB bookbub.com/authors/dawn-brower

f facebook.com/1DawnBrower

🐦 twitter.com/1DawnBrower

📷 instagram.com/1DawnBrower

g goodreads.com/dawnbrower

If It's Love (Amanda Mariel)

Odds of Love (Dawn Brower)

Believe In Love (Amanda Mariel)

Chance of Love (Dawn Brower)

Love and Holly (Amanda Mariel)

Love and Mistletoe (Dawn Brower

Bluestockings Defying Rogues

When An Earl Turns Wicked

A Lady Hoyden's Secret

One Wicked Kiss

Earl In Trouble

All the Ladies Love Coventry

One Less Scandalous Earl

Confessions of a Hellion

Coming Soon

The Vixen in Red

Marsden Descendants

Rebellious Angel

Tempting An American Princess

How to Kiss a Debutante

Loving an America Spy

Scheming with My Duke

Secluded with My Hellion

Coming Soon

Secrets of My Beloved

Spying on My Scoundrel

Shocked by My Vixen

Heart's Intent

One Heart to Give

Unveiled Hearts

Heart of the Moment

Kiss My Heart Goodbye

Heart in Waiting

Broken Curses

The Enchanted Princess

The Bespelled Knight

The Magical Hunt

Ever Beloved

Forever My Earl

Always My Viscount

Infinitely My Marquess

EternallyMyDuke

Kismet Bay

AFTERWORD

Thank you so much for taking the time to read my book.
Your opinion matters!
Please take a moment to review this book on your favorite review site and share your opinion with fellow readers.

www.authordawnbrower.com

ACKNOWLEDGMENTS

A huge thanks to those that helped me make this all sparkly; Victoria for helping with the fine tuning, Liz for reading my rough draft, and Christina for cleaning it up. Without you this book would be riddled with errors. Thanks for all that you did to make it even better.